Meredith's Wolf

ISBN-13: 978-0-9859255-9-8
ISBN-10: 0-9859255-9-0

First printing, February, 2014

Front cover photo by Holly Kuchera

Cover design by ThomasMax

Published by:

ThomasMax Publishing
P.O. Box 250054
Atlanta, GA 30325
thomasmax.com

Meredith's Wolf

by Judith Barban

ThomasMax
Your Publisher
For The 21st Century

Acknowledgments

This book would not have been possible without the generous advice of professionals and the brilliant suggestions of early readers and friends. Among those professionals are Trevor and Jody Dick who own and operate the first-rate Bolton Lake Fishing and Hunting Lodge in northeastern Manitoba, Canada. The waters of Bolton Lake have provided anglers like myself with trophy walleye, northern pike, and lake trout year after year. Their lodge served as the model for my fictional one.

I am indebted to two floatplane pilots for sharing their expertise with me: Kevin Walsten of Walsten Lodge and Outposts based in Kenora, Ontario, outfitter and heroic bush pilot, for advice and wilderness opportunity; Pat Patterson, neighbor and flight instructor, for guiding me through the mechanics of seaplane operations and reviewing the appropriate sections of the book.

Special tahnks to Richard Hebel, owner of the great Cobham River Lodge in Manitoba, whose son did in fact find a wilderness wolf pup and raised him to adulthood—the inspiration for my story.

As I read portions of each chapter at our meetings, the sharp eyes and ears and astute insights of the members of my two writers' groups contributed significantly to the quality of the work. Thank you all for your patience and enthusiastic support.

I am forever grateful to ThomasMax Publishing and to my editor Lee Clevenger for his faith in me as a writer, for the timely manner in which he expedites the work, for his advice, for his always positive attitude, and for his friendship.

A huge thank-you to my husband Gene for his time to read, to re-read, then to make tactful suggestions, all of which were right on the mark.

— J.B.

*To all tribes and clans
of Native Americans
and First Nations people
of North America
whose land
my forefathers took away*

About the Author

A native of Atlanta, GA, Judith Barban has garnered numerous awards for her novels, short stories, and poetry. Her first novel, *Poplar River*, won the coveted "You Are Published" award sponsored by the Southeastern Writers' Association. Set in the pristine wilderness, this work and its sequel, *Meredith's Wolf*, transport readers into a world of unspoiled natural beauty and wildlife, a world fraught with danger, suspense, and romance. An illustrated poetry collection, *Crown Jewels,* contains a number of top prize-winning poems. She is a popular guest speaker at book clubs, libraries, universities, and civic organizations.

Judith holds Bachelors and Masters Degrees in French and Piano Performance as well as a PhD in Medieval French Language and Literature. Honors include Phi Beta Kappa and a Fulbright Grant to France. She is widely published in scholarly journals in both the fields of music and French literature. An edition and first-ever translation of a 13th-century manuscript, *The Life of Saint Audrey: A Text by Marie de France* has distinguished her in the area of Medieval Studies.

Judith and her husband Eugene, a concert pianist, live in Tega Cay, SC, with their "tuxedo" cat, Steinway. They spend a part of every summer fishing and camping in the Canadian wilderness.

Chapter One

After take-off and leveling-out, it was smooth flying through a cloudless sky. Calm air kept the floatplane steady. Meredith relaxed her grip on the control wheel, checked out the altimeter and the air speed indicator—three thousand feet, 90 knots.

She sat back and began to plan how she would go about finding her wolf once she reached the spot where she and Bobby had released him back into the wild. From the cockpit the Canadian wilderness stretched to the horizon all around her. Natural lakes and pristine forests carpeted the earth below. She loved the beauty that lay beneath her, especially this God's-eye view of it.

A sudden series of air pockets bounced the Cessna around. Meredith jumped to full alert. Static on the radio blurred the emission, making it incomprehensible over her headphones. She turned up the volume. Through the buzzes and pops she was able to decipher enough to learn that storm cells had formed on her flight path and that she should divert to the east. Even while listening to the message, Meredith spotted dark clouds in front of her. The turbulence increased. She dipped the right wing, banking to begin her diversion. It was too little too late. The Cessna flew directly into the storm.

The wind and rain buffeted the light aircraft, causing it to yaw and pitch wildly. She flinched at every clap of thunder and struggled to maintain control—of her emotions as well as the plane. Piloting under Visual Flight Rules, she must be able to see the ground, but clouds and pounding rain obscured everything.

I must think clearly and not panic.

A flash of lightning and a sharp crack. The radio went dead.

I can't worry about that now. I've got to get out of this storm.

It was much worse than she had thought and seemed to cover a wide area. There was no way she could go around it. She would have to drop below it and hope that conditions closer to the ground would be better.

And they were. As soon as she could discern tree tops and small lakes, she felt a little relief. The ceiling was low, but she could manage for a while at this altitude. Until she realized that she had completely lost her bearings. At a low level nothing resembled the navigation charts she had studied so long and hard.

When it gets safe to climb back to three thousand feet I'll be okay. I'll know where I am. I may be only sixteen, but I'm a licensed bush pilot, and I can handle this weather.

Straight ahead a large body of water was coming into view. At least that's what it looked like through the haze of rain and slower propeller speed. She needed to climb up a little. Then maybe she could re-orient herself. Meredith opened the throttle. The engine misfired and failed.

"What's wrong with you?" she asked the engine, as if it could understand her fear and frustration. She tried everything she could think of, starting it again and again. Nothing but sputters. There was no other alternative—she would have to land without power on the lake that loomed before her.

"Make sure the rudders are up. Wing flaps at 30 degrees. Master switch off. Doors unlatched." Speaking aloud to bolster her confidence, Meredith went through the litany of what Bobby and Paul had taught to do in a forced landing without power. She had to do it twice before to get her license—under ideal conditions. She strapped on a life jacket. As the Cessna approached the water, she had done all she knew to do. Only one recourse remained:

"Dear God, forgive my deceitfulness. I never should have tried this while Mama and Bobby were away from the lodge. Help me to land safely." That's all the time she had. The left float hit the water. Hard.

The force of the uneven impact made the plane tilt sharply and veer to the left. The wingtip cut through the air only inches above the surface.

"I'm going to capsize!"

Acting out of instinct, Meredith fixed the ailerons to direct as much air as possible onto the right wing and off of the left and set the rudder to straighten the aircraft. After a few terrifying seconds the left wing rose and the right float touched down. The wings straightened out, horizontal again. Surface speed slowed enough for her to use the float rudders and regain directional control.

"Thank you, God, oh thank you!" Despite shaking hands and arms, she maneuvered the powerless aircraft toward a sheltered bay. The

Cessna came to a halt, mired in loamy weed beds about ten feet from shore.

At first Meredith couldn't move. She had regained control of the plane but not the violent trembling of her body. Her heart was beating so forcefully it felt poised in the back of her throat, ready to be expelled with the contents of her stomach. She opened the door just in time. Even after the stomach had emptied itself of all juices and acids, the heaving spasms continued.

When her breathing became regular again, Meredith looked at her watch then gave herself audible commands. She had split into two people. The Petrified Passenger and the Captain in Control. "Document the forced landing. Switch on the emergency locator transmitter. Check the aircraft for damage. Assess your situation." The standard pilot logbook and operating handbook had slid out from beneath the seat and were now under her feet. She found a pen and wrote, almost illegibly, a two-sentence account of the landing.

Lost power and radio in storm. Forced landing on unidentified lake in northeast quadrant of Manitoba.

Crawling to the rear of the plane, she switched on the Emergency Locator Transmitter. No light. No signal. *Why wasn't it working? The lightning? Maybe I'm doing something wrong.* She had never paid attention to it before. Bobby or Paul had always turned it on before each flight. Why hadn't she? She knew where it was and what it did, but how could she know if it were functioning properly? She went back to the cockpit and speed-read the section on the ELT in the Pilot's Operating Handbook. It offered no explanation. She left the switch on in hopes it might start working.

Inspection of the left wing and float for possible damage came next. She removed her boots and socks, rolled up her jeans as far as possible and stepped down onto the pontoon then into the thigh-deep water. The early fall temperatures had not dropped enough to suck the summer warmth from the shallow bay. The left float appeared intact. She sloshed through the weeds to the end of the wing. No damage there. The plane seemed flight-worthy. That discovery brought some comfort, and the two Merediths began to fuse back into one.

"Good old Cessna! You saved my life." Meredith patted the strut framework that held the appropriate landing equipment—floats, wheels, or skis. She was licensed for the first two but not the skis. "I'll get Bobby or Paul to teach me how to land on snow. It can't be that different. Nothing could be scarier than what I just went through." She felt good about the fact that she had successfully negotiated her way through a storm and a difficult landing with low visibility and no power and without damage to the plane.

"Let's get this bird back into the air."

She sloshed out to the tail and began to push, wading in a semi-circle, to turn the plane around. It took a lot of muscle power to walk in the ankle-deep mud and numerous grunts and groans to dislodge the plane from the grip of the weeds. Finally it faced open water. She shimmied up onto a float, crawled along to reach the cross-bars and still-open pilot's door, and climbed into the cockpit. She sat for a moment to catch her breath then pressed the starter. The engine coughed, the propellers took a half turn, but no luck. Another try. Nothing. She checked the gauges. *There is plenty of fuel, there was no damage to the plane, why won't it start?*

This was not good. If the engine wouldn't start, she'd have to send out an emergency message via radio, and that would alert Royal Canadian Mounted Police Air Services who would dispatch a Sea and Air Rescue plane. Her mother and Bobby would never forgive her for sneaking off alone. No, the May Day signal would be her last resort.

Then she remembered. The radio was dead. *With the engine, the radio, and the transmitter not functioning, how am I going to get out of here? I don't even know where I am. What lake is this? I don't know its name, but I do have a map and may be able to figure out its coordinates.* But without a radio, there was no way to communicate with any rescuers. The gravity of her situation was taking shape in her mind. Fear spread like a brush fire through her body. Her throat closed, but her eyes were latched wide open. She was wet, cold, confused, and lost—in the middle of the wilderness where she would have to survive until somebody found her—if anybody ever found her. She brought her palms to her face, releasing her desperation in tears and sobs.

Feeling sorry for herself didn't last long. She was made of tougher mettle than that. Bobby was. Her mother, too.

"I'd better take stock." The voice of the Captain in Control returned.

She spent the next few minutes scouring every inch of the plane's cabin, piling everything of any possible utility in the copilot's seat: a first aid kit, a blanket, a small box of matches, an old magazine—*Canada Fishing*, a coil of good marine rope, and a fishing rod rigged with line and an attached lure—a silver spoon with hanging treble hook. Bobby. Always prepared to fish. And he had taught her. How many times she and her step-father had fished together on Baldwin Lake. If only she hadn't been so foolhardy. She fought back more tears.

"I will survive this, I will!"

The surge of determination brought with it an idea.

"Build a bonfire. I have matches."

The storm had moved on. Clouds were thinning. The plane had drifted backwards into the weed beds, giving her easy access to shore. With the coil of rope around one shoulder, she waded in, taking care to keep the matches and the magazine dry. First order of business was to secure the plane. She tied one end of the rope to a mooring line attached to the landing gear and the other to a convenient white pine. A short distance into the bush she found enough dead wood and dry tinder. Piling it up on a large flat rock at the water's edge, she crumpled several pages of the magazine, placed the smaller, drier wood on top, and lit the fire. Fanned by the wind, it burned quickly and required constant feeding, necessitating numerous trips in and out of the bush to hunt for dry wood. When the last of the magazine had burned, cover and all, Meredith stood watching the embers die out. Light wind lifted charred remnants of *Canada Fishing* into the air.

"Maybe somebody saw it and will come." But it was a faint hope, for the fire never really got going.

She climbed back into the plane, exchanged her wet jeans and panties for the fresh underwear her mother had trained her always to take along and hung the jeans on a grommet. She donned the extra sweater stuffed in her backpack and wrapped the blanket around her bottom half. She ate one of two turkey sandwiches she had made that morning, and waited. The rest of the day. The clouds cleared completely. The sun sank red behind the trees. Light faded. Meredith crawled into the tail of the plane. Using her backpack as a pillow, she curled into a fetal position, pulled the blanket up, and slept.

Sometime during the short, dark hours of the Canadian summer night, Meredith woke up abruptly. Something bumped against the plane. She listened. A creature, a large creature, was moving around outside the aircraft. The water swished, the plane was jostled. There was a sound of an animal breathing and gnawing on metal. The water swished again. The girl dared not move or breathe. The scraping of teeth against metal continued, stopped then started again. She had lived through the longest day of her life only to endure this, the longest night. She lay perfectly still listening. In the dead quiet of the forest night, it sounded like the plane was being torn apart.

Can he get inside? Bears have been known to tear doors off automobiles in national parks. I do have food in here. Can he smell it? Is he after it? Or is he after me?

Visions of her own body being dragged through the bush, her head clenched between the upper and lower fangs of a huge bear, sent bolts of terror through her nervous system. Her chest tightened, forcing her to take shallow, rapid breaths.

The minutes of gnawing lasted years in her mind. But the noises finally stopped, and the plane and the water became still again. She should try to go back to sleep. She closed her eyes but they immediately snapped open. Her body was in survival mode. No way could she sleep. She would have to lie there and wait until it got light enough. Then she would muster her courage, sit up, and look out.

* * *

A wedge of sunlight streaming across her face woke Meredith. She sat up, bumping her head hard against the sloping roof of the tail section. The reality of her situation hit her just as hard.

"How will I ever get out of here? If I don't die here, Mama and Bobby are going to kill me. What ever possessed me to think I could fly up and find Wolfie all by myself!"

Her shoulders shook and tears came. She wiped her cheeks with the back of her hand, sniffled a few times until finally the Captain in Control took charge of the Little Girl Lost.

"I've got to figure this out for myself. First things first. I'll eat one of the bacon biscuits I fixed for Wolfie then check out the damage done by that animal—a bear, no doubt."

Throwing aside the blanket, she opened her backpack, unwrapped the package of biscuits, and devoured one in two bites.

"Sorry, Wolfie." She dusted the biscuit crumbs from her hands.

Even with the sun now high above the horizon, the air was chilled. Meredith breathed deeply the crisp morning air and slipped on her jacket.

She bent forward and crawled toward the cockpit. Leaning a forearm on each of the pilots' seatbacks, she bent to look out the front windows. Morning clouds formed parallel lines that resembled pink jet trails against the light blue morning sky, the promise of good weather. A mist hung above the water like the vague memory of a dream rapidly dissipating into nothingness.

Dressed in panties and her jacket, she sat in the cockpit, opened the door on the pilot's side, and slid into the thigh-deep water. Silt and loam oozed through her toes. From where she stood she could see the entire left side of the plane.

"No damage here." She slogged around past the propellers and examined them in passing. They seemed fine. On the right side she found what she was looking for.

"Just as I thought. A bear, for sure." She surveyed the holes chewed into the right pontoon.

"He probably thought the float was a giant northern pike, or else he smelled something edible in one of the pontoon storage compartments."

Trudging on around for a closer look, she determined that the holes were in only one compartment. "That's not too bad." Then she found holes in the float rudders. "But that's not too good," she said, wondering if they would impair the steering of the plane on water. She knew there could be holes underneath, possibly enough to fill the float with too much water and make it unsafe for take-off.

She sloshed back around to the open door and climbed the crossbars between the struts.

"Now let's get off the water and into the air." Hoping that whatever caused the engine failure had miraculously resolved itself, Meredith adjusted the throttle and tried the starter. A low grinding sound, one revolution of the propeller, then nothing.

"I'm going to get this thing started."

But she couldn't, try after try.

"The radio. It's surely working now."

But it wasn't.

Meredith located the Pilot's Operating Handbook and read everything she could find about engine failure but it provided no help. Under "Emergency Procedures" she learned that every plane should be equipped with flares.

"Flares! I'm sure Bobby has them here somewhere. I'll find them."

But she didn't.

In her frustration she reached in her backpack and pulled out what remained of her food—one bacon biscuit and one turkey sandwich. She ate the sandwich.

"Okay. There's only one thing left to do. Build a bonfire and keep it going until somebody spots it. At least I have matches," she told herself, checking her jacket pocket, just to be sure the matches were still there.

She stuffed thick socks into her hiking boots, tied the laces of one shoe to the laces of the other and hung them around her neck. Sticking the one remaining bacon biscuit in her jeans pocket, she draped the jeans over her shoulders and tied the legs together in front. Then, donning the backpack, she stood at the door of the Cessna like a skydiver about to plunge into the void, simultaneously experiencing the thrill of adventure and fear of death.

"'You can do it, Muffin. Just keep focused. Think clearly.'" She repeated the phrase that Bobby often used to give her courage when teaching her to fly. She slipped into the water.

Once on shore she put on jeans, socks, and boots. Surveying the area, she decided that the place where she moored the plane was too sheltered.

"That's why nobody saw the fire yesterday. We'd better scout around for a place with more visibility." She had discovered that talking to herself aloud in the first person plural made her feel less alone and bolstered her confidence. "Let's follow the shoreline until we find just the right spot for our signal fire."

The going was not easy. In places jumbles of large rocks jutted up at odd angles. In others the land dropped straight down to the water. Fallen trees often blocked the way. The footing was at times marshy, at times rocky. Meredith slowly but steadily made her way, clinging to limbs, bushes, and vines, scooting along on her backside, and scrabbling over boulders. Around a bend in the shoreline Meredith found what she thought must be the ideal location for a bonfire. A peninsula with a large flat rock at the end extended well out into the water. A curving strip of sand formed a narrow beach. Bits of bone-dry poplar bark curls lay scattered about the beach just waiting to be used as a fire-starter.

"Perfect. A fire on that point can't be missed." She sat her backpack down on the sand. "Okay, now we gather as much firewood as possible."

She hadn't thought that wood-gathering could be so strenuous or so time-consuming. In the bush she found plenty of dry wood of various sizes but had nothing to carry it with except her bare hands. She tried hauling it in her jacket but then she couldn't watch her steps and fell several times. After a great deal of physical exertion and sheer will-power, three huge piles of firewood stood next to a ring of stones on top of the flat rock—kindling, medium, and thick. Then she prepared the fire, laying it in her best Girl Scout fashion. Exhausted and hungry, she sat down on the rock, reached in her jeans pocket for the last biscuit, but it was not there.

"Must have fallen into the water when I had the jeans dangling over my back. That was dumb of me. We've got to start thinking more clearly before we act."

Knowing that once she struck the match, she would be a full-time fire steward, she cupped her hands behind her head and lay back on the rock. A herring gull cart-wheeled overhead, circling the bay, squealing and cawing. Meredith sat up on her elbows to watch. *Squee-caw-caw-caw*. As she followed the bird's flight path, a feeling of deja-vu came over her. She had been too occupied with wood-gathering to take careful note of the area. Now she took the entire scene in—the curve of the sandy beach, the configuration of the trees and bushes, the angle of the rocky peninsula. She knew without a shadow of a doubt.

"This is where we left him! This is Wolfie's lake!"

Chapter Two

The night Wolfie came to Baldwin Lake the moon had risen full and orange, looking like a gigantic planet about to collide with the earth. At the other end of the camp, the sun had dropped below the horizon, leaving a pink luminescence against which the leafless aspen poplars formed tall, stark silhouettes. The wind was low over the lake creating strong ripples that lapped against the shore like a thirsty animal. Sitting on a boulder beside the water, Meredith heard a sound above the hypnotic pattern of the waves. Something was whimpering. She swiveled to face the main lodge building, removed the knit cap from her unruly curls, and cocked her head in the manner of a gray jay to listen. The sound came from the bushes surrounding the deck, near the stairs. Having spent five summers here, the fourteen-year-old had learned to move with care in the still of the Canadian wilderness. She approached with steps as slow and silent as possible, then, stuffing her cap into a jacket pocket, gently parted the shrubs. Meredith took her first look at Wolfie.

Without lifting his head he raised his eyes to her. At that moment, despite the yellow mucous that ran from the inward corners, the pathos emanating from the cerulean blue irises embedded itself instantly and completely in Meredith's heart. The scrawny animal seemed to be saying to her, "Help me, and I will love you forever."

"Oh, you sweet little thing. I'll take care of you. Please let me pick you up and love you."

She inched toward the pup on her knees, not wanting to startle him or appear threatening. She cautiously stretched out a hand, palm downward, and held it in front of the animal's nose. His nostrils flared. Still the creature did not lift its head. Through the grimy fur the emaciated body trembled.

She touched his forehead, ran her fingertips along his bony neck and back. The pup didn't flinch. The more she stroked the gaunt body, the more she wanted that pup worse than anything in the world.

"You're hungry, aren't you? And you need a bath. Come on with me now."

She slid one hand under the pup's ribs and gently lifted him. With the other hand she braced him and drew him to her chest. Her chin instinctively nestled against the top of his head. She could feel the trembling. But he didn't struggle to free himself.

"Don't be afraid. You're so weak . . . and helpless. You need me. And I need you."

Still on her knees, she began rocking back and forth to calm the animal while allowing the tide of affection for him to flow from her heart into his. When the pup closed his eyes and laid his head in the crook of her elbow, she slowly stood up.

"Easy now. We're going inside where you will be safe."

Making every step as smooth as possible, she carried the pup up the stairs and across the deck to the glass doorway of the lodge dining room. Cradling the pathetic creature in one arm, with her free hand and one knee she slid open the door and crossed the threshold carrying her prized possession into the lives of her mother, step-father, and all those who, over the next two years, would spend time at Baldwin Lake Fishing and Hunting Lodge.

The animal, eyes wide with fear, was still shaking but no longer whining. She switched him to a double-arm position, steadied her pace, walked into the lodge office, and stood with the pup, as radiant as a madonna and child.

"Mama, look what I found."

"What in the world have you got there?" Karen set her pen down.

"It's a puppy. Can I keep him?"

Her mother got up from the desk and came over for a closer look. A woman in her mid thirties, she looked ten years younger. Her long brown hair was held gently in place at the nape of her neck by a covered elastic band. Wispy strands fell over her forehead and temples and softened the sharpness of her clear green eyes. Tight jeans and a black turtleneck enhanced her slender figure. She still possessed all the charm and gentility of the small-town South Carolina girl she was before she married. To Meredith, she was the most beautiful woman in the world, especially when she swirled out on a stage in some extraordinary, sparkling gown to play the piano.

"Sugar Baby, go get Bobby. He's in the kitchen fixing a window. I think he'd better have a look at this thing." She took the little fellow from her daughter and, slipping her hands under his shoulders, held him up, legs dangling. "He's awfully thin."

Meredith adored "Uncle Bobby." That's what she had always called her father's cousin, even after he became her stepfather. But more then these, he was her best friend and the greatest influence on her life. She was eager for him to see the new acquisition, in which she was already beginning to take great pride.

"It's a wolf pup. Couldn't be much more than six weeks old. His eyes are still blue." Bobby knew the wilderness and its inhabitants. He had been a fishing and hunting outfitter for years and now owned and operated a first-class lodge in northern Manitoba. "The mother and the rest of the litter must be dead. Otherwise this little guy wouldn't have wandered away by himself. And he's starving. I'm not sure he'll make it."

"Oh, please, can we try to save him?"

"Of course we will. Run to the storage room and get an empty box to put him in, then we'll heat some milk."

* * *

Wolfie survived and spent a blissful puppyhood and young adult life at Baldwin Lake Lodge. His eyes turned a brilliant amber-gold. His brindled fur thickened. He quickly became everyone's pet—Karen's, Bobby's, the guides', the fishermen's, and the hunters'. Despite all the attention, he remained naturally shy around people—with one exception: he was Meredith's constant companion. During the long, snowy winters back home in Winnipeg the two played together, ate together, and slept together. They rode together in the back seat of the Cessna floatplane that took the family up north to the lake at ice-out every spring.

Pictures of Meredith and Wolfie appeared in all the publicity brochures for the lodge: one of the girl with her arm around the wolf's neck, both of them bright-eyed and smiling, another of Wolfie licking the girl's face, and another of the two of them snuggled up together napping under a blue spruce, with Wolfie's lanky legs stretching toward the camera. Returning lodge guests brought him rawhide chews, nylon bones, dog biscuits, and various canine toys. A few even gave him doggie sweaters, blue or yellow, with a little red heart knitted in. In spite of the family's ban on a wolf in the dining room while guests were eating, Wolfie got many a handout from Meredith and the camp cook in the kitchen. He was no longer thin.

"Wolfie" wasn't his real name. From Tom, the Ojibwe elder who worked part time at the lodge whenever Bobby needed extra help, Meredith learned the word for wolf in the Anishinaabe language, "maengun," so Maengun he was. She liked the fact that his name started with the letter M like both her first and last, Meredith Marsten, but the guides—most of them from Quebec or Nova Scotia—and the fishermen had trouble pronouncing it or even remembering it. In time "Wolfie" won out.

As the wolf—and the child—matured, he and Meredith switched roles. He became her nanny and protector. In the mornings he would sit by the bed looking at her sleeping face until her eyes opened. Then he would fetch her shoes from wherever she had kicked them off, drop them beside the bed, and stand there, tongue hanging, panting in expectation of another fine day together. In good weather the two of them would go down to the dock, hop in the owner's boat, and motor out onto the lake to fish. The animal watched her every move. He scanned the water for fish. He regularly sniffed the air, as if checking for any sign of change in the weather that could endanger his protégé. Her parents entrusted the teenager's care to the wolf as long as they stayed in sight of the camp. Meredith and Wolfie abided by the stipulation.

Bobby had helped her perfect her fishing and boating skills. She was an enthusiastic disciple and a fast learner. For years she had hounded him for flying lessons until finally he promised to start after her sixteenth birthday. She was bound and determined to be just like Uncle Bobby, to know the wilderness as he did, to do all the amazing things he could do. She dressed like him. Even puberty hadn't changed her mind. She was completely natural, no make-up, no fad hair or clothing styles, no obsession with electronic gadgets. Her fashion statement consisted of tangled curls, stained jeans, a faded flannel shirt, and scuffed hiking boots. And, so far, no teenage infatuations. Not counting the three hundred-or-so fishermen at the lodge over the summer, Wolfie and Bobby were the males in her life. And they filled it.

* * *

Meredith loved showing Wolfie off to the fisherman at the lodge. She was permitted to bring him into the dining room when the guys gathered before dinner for cocktails and hors-d'oeuvres after their long day out on the lake. Because his natural shyness around people made him uncomfortable with the men, he stuck close to his mistress, walking and sitting by her side at all times. The fishermen or hunters asked the usual questions, which Meredith enjoyed answering:

"That a real wolf?"

"Male or female?"

"You catch him with a trap?"

"How long have you had him?"

"Can I pet him, or will he bite?"

"He gotta name? . . . Maen- . . . Yeah, well, I'll just call him Wolfie."

"Okay if I save some tidbits for him from my plate?"

"Do you feed him dog food or live animals?"

"Do a lot of Canadian kids have wolves as pets?"

Meredith was proud of her wolf and reveled in the attention paid him by the lodge guests. Some evenings during the dinner hour, since he was banned from the dining room at that time, she would take Wolfie out in the boat to fish in front of the lodge where the guests could admire her and her pet while they enjoyed their prime rib or some other copious feast. Every morning she and Wolfie put in an appearance on the dock while the fishermen and guides prepared to set out for the day. With the wolf standing beside her, excitement in his shining eyes and swishing tail, she waved goodbye to each boat when the guide motored away.

She was taken by surprise one evening after dinner when one of the guests, a rather distinguished middle-aged man with dark hair graying at the temples and a trim physique, approached her and Wolfie during their pre-bedtime walk.

"How much would you take for that wolf? I'd sure like to buy him."

"Well, I'm sorry, but he's not for sale."

"Price is no object."

"He's just not for sale."

"What if I said you could spend time with him in my home anytime you wanted to? I live in Chicago—I'd even pay the airfare whenever you flew down. I'd give you the grand tour of the Windy City. We'd have fun. I'd enjoy your company."

During the conversation Wolfie had been sitting on his haunches watching a pair of water thrushes swoop over the lake. He swung his head around, stood up, raised the hackles on his back, and gave a low, menacing growl.

Meredith understood the wolf's message. *Yes, Wolfie, I agree. Something is not right about this situation. This guy's got more in mind than just owning a wolf. The jerk.*

"I'm not the least bit interested." Meredith spoke with her most disgusted tone. "Excuse me, we have to go in now."

She tossed back her tawny curls, lifted her chin in a defiant manner, and stomped back to the main building, up the steps to the deck, and in through the sliding glass door, closing it with a firm purpose, almost slamming it on Wolfie's tail. The fishermen were always friendly toward her, but never had one tried to trick her into getting too close.

He wanted to use Wolfie. He must think I'm stupid . . . or really naïve.

Meredith went to the bar and fished a Diet Coke out of the ice bin. The wolf continued to watch through the glass door, growling softly until the man disappeared into his cabin.

"Thanks for warning me. We'll have to keep our distance from that one, won't we, boy?" Meredith told Wolfie when she slipped under the covers in their tiny once-a-storage-closet bedroom.

* * *

Karen stood at the glass door of the dining room looking out at the lake. This was her favorite time of the day. Breakfast was over, tables cleared and reset for dinner. The guests and guides were all out on the lake, scattered to the four winds, out of sight. After the spate of activity serving the morning meal to twenty-four boisterous fishermen, a quiet solitude settled over the camp. Kitchen noises had diminished, nothing left but the whirr of the dishwasher, barely audible where she was in the main room. She saw the two women hired as housekeepers head off to their duties in the guests' cabins, making beds, cleaning bathrooms, and collecting trash.

Taking a sip of coffee from her mug, she spotted Meredith and her wolf making their way back from the pier where they had seen the guests and guides off for the day. They veered off the boardwalk, headed to the water's edge, and began a game of fetch. Karen smiled as she watched the two of them. Wolfie was not always cooperative, preferring to run away with the stick or lie down and chew on it.

"What's so fascinating out there?" Bobby came up behind her, wrapped his arms around her waist, touching his cheek to hers.

"Just watching Meredith's futile efforts to teach Wolfie to fetch."

"They'll work it out."

"I'm not sure it's good for her to spend so much time with that wolf," Karen sighed. "He's company for her, but, you know, she turned sixteen her last birthday. She's outgoing with all the guests here, but she's never had many close friends her own age, always been kind of a loner—until she found Wolfie."

"I think it's great that the two of them are together. Rescued animals have a way of understanding and are forever devoted to the one who saved them. It's a strong bond, Karen."

"I know you're right, Honey, but still . . . I worry that she's not growing up socially well-rounded."

Bobby spun her around to face him.

"She's growing up just fine. Besides, it's about time to release the wolf back into the wild. You're the one I'm concerned about. You're stuck working at a fishing lodge four months out of the year and your time at home is spent practicing and traveling to give concerts. When do you get to enjoy the company of women your age?"

"I love my life the way it is, Bobby."

"So does she."

"Yes, she does." Karen smiled, leaned forward, and kissed her husband lightly on the lips. Bobby could always make her see things logically, just like her father did.

"I came to tell you that I just got off the phone to Ralph Haygood. He's decided he wants to go ahead with the purchase of three of our outposts. He plans a lot of upgrades—like solar power, new windows, appliances. Wants to get all the papers signed before the end of the season so he can start getting the cabins ready for next year before the bad weather sets in."

"That'll be a relief—to have only two outposts to deal with."

"We're setting up a meeting in Winnipeg with an attorney and the provincial representative in a few weeks. Would you like to come along?"

"Do you need me to be at this meeting?"

"Not really. But I just thought you might like to do some shopping or get your hair done—give you a break before we start closing down for the winter."

"You know I don't ever have my hair done, silly. But shopping sounds good. Can we both be absent from the lodge?"

"I think we can arrange it. Trust me. See you at lunch."

Bobby went back to the office. Karen opened the glass door and stepped out into the crisp Canadian air. She set her mug of by-now-cold coffee down on the railing, propped her elbows on each side of it and, resting her chin on her knuckles, looked out at the mist hovering over the lake. Both the lake and the forest were shrouded in gray. Darkening morning clouds signaled approaching rainstorms. Karen thought about Bobby's proposal and decided to take him up on it. She needed this trip to Winnipeg, but shopping was not on her mind. A sudden gust of wind swept in from the north, bringing with it an ominous chill that troubled both the gray water and Karen's spirit.

* * *

Wolfie knew where his toys were kept. He made periodic trips to the big basket in one corner of the owner's living room just to check on them, or grab one for a little tossing, chewing, and shaking. He enjoyed playing with them by himself, but when Meredith sat down beside him and teased him with one, well, that was special—and a lot more fun.

He stuck his muzzle in the basket and pulled out a hard rubber bone.

I'm going to take this to her. I don't often see her chewing on things, but I bet she would like this one today.

He brought his head out of the basket. With the bone hanging down one side of his mouth, he ran to Meredith's room and stopped at the open door.

Not here.

He backed out and headed toward the hall leading to the main dining room, bone drooping and saliva dripping. He paused at the entrance and listened to the general hubbub.

The fishermen are back. Maybe I'd better not do this now. She's busy with them anyway.

He dropped the bone and turned to go back down the hall to the owner's apartment.

"There you are, Wolfie. Come get a treat. Emil has prepared some yummy hors-d'oeuvres."

When he heard her voice he couldn't help but respond. He threaded his way through the guests gathered at the bar and found her seated on a barstool nibbling on the yummies. They did smell good, better than the fake bone he had planned to offer her. She lowered her hand and held a piece of something in front of his nose. Wolfie didn't know or care what it was. He ate it because she gave it to him.

He sat patiently at her heels, waiting for dinner to be served. Then all these people would go to their tables and start eating. He and Meredith would take the boat out in front of the lodge and fish awhile, then come back, cross the almost-empty guests' dining room, go through the kitchen to the small dining room in back. Wolfie liked that better. Just his lodge family. Even the guides had already eaten and were out gassing up their boats for tomorrow's long day on the lake. He could sneak into the large room and get illegal hand-outs from lingering guests, but he felt more comfortable in the back room. As usual, he would lie down in one corner, watching and listening.

During the family meal Wolfie noticed Bobby speaking in a low voice to Meredith. Then both of them turned to look at him. He saw Meredith shake her head. She sat staring at her plate then rose from the table and went to the door of the owner's apartment.

Something Bobby said has upset her.

"Come, Wolfie, come with me, boy."

He followed her into the closet-bedroom. She sat on the floor, placed her hands on each side of his neck behind his ears, held his head erect, and looked him in the eyes.

"You are my best friend, Wolfie. I will always love you. Don't ever forget that. Don't ever forget me. Promise me you won't."

He didn't fully understand what she was telling him, but her voice was sweet and soft and that made him happy. His tail brushed back and forth over the wooden floor. Until he noticed that she was crying.

* * *

"What in the world did you say to Meredith that upset her at the table? She didn't even eat her supper." Karen and Bobby were closing up the office for the night. Tomorrow was Saturday—change-over day when this week's guests departed and the new ones arrived. There was always a lot of paperwork—bar and tackle-shop bills to be tabulated, invoices prepared. She slipped the passenger list she had prepared for the Big Bear Airlines pilot into the desk drawer and clicked on the answering machine.

Bobby closed the accounts file and turned off the computer. "She said that Wolfie wants to go outside at night now. I told her we have heard him howling and reminded her that one day soon he'll have to be returned to the wild. She's known that from the beginning. It's hard for her to accept, but I know she wants to do what's best for the wolf."

"When do you plan to do it?"

"Well, don't you think it would be best if Muffin decided that for herself?"

"Then we'll keep the wolf forever."

"No, she realizes that having a mature wolf at home in Winnipeg is becoming problematic. Besides, she knows it's illegal. I had to pull some strings to get a temporary permit to keep him. Even though he acts like one, Wolfie's not a domestic animal. He's not a dog. Neighbors are concerned for the safety of their children and their pets. We could be liable."

"I never thought about it that way. He's always been so shy and well behaved. Except for the time or two he lifted his leg in the house to mark his territory. I guess I have been treating him like a domestic animal, too. You'll have to admit he's sweet, and like you said, devoted to Meredith."

"He is. But to answer your question, he should be released and resettled before we shut down the camp this year. We have to obey provincial law. That's why I mentioned it at dinner."

Karen tightened her lips. "I know she'll comply, but it's really going to hurt." She sighed and said under her breath, "It already has." She stood up and snapped off the office light.

* * *

Meredith couldn't sleep. Wolfie had settled on the rug beside her bed. She could hear the soft, regular cadence of his breathing. She lay still so as not to disturb him. Tears ran along a downward track that crossed her temples and soaked into the brown curls that covered her ears.

I know he needs to be back in the wild. He was made to run with a pack, to hunt and kill, to feed himself, and to follow his instincts. He needs to become a real wolf, not a pet. I know all that. But it's going to be so hard to let him go.

She wiped her wet temples with the top of the sheet and turned to face the wall, her back to Wolfie.

I'll always have the memories of everything we've shared. I'll always remember that first moment I saw him, how pathetic and sweet he was.

The thought of their first encounter released a stream of puppy images that passed in review—feeding him from a baby bottle, running meat through a grinder and filling his bowl with it then watching him gobble it up, presenting him with new toys from the guests, many of which were instantly torn to shreds. She smiled as she thought of his first encounter with a duck. He lowered the front half of his body and yipped so hard he was propelled backwards. In her mind she saw him burying bones then digging them up. She remembered the days they fished together—Wolfie sitting in the prow watching her bait the hook, cast, and pull in a fish. Sometimes he would try to grab a wiggling walleye before she could get it back into the water. She recalled the nights early on when she had slept with the wolf pup in her arms, inhaling the natural aroma of his thick, wild fur and feeling the rapid beat of his feral heart.

The relived moments gradually transformed themselves into dream images and the girl and her wolf slept deeply through the short Canadian night.

* * *

So the dreaded day is coming soon, Meredith thought. It had been a little more than two years since the wolf pup's appearance at Baldwin Lake. She was helping the camp waitress set tables for dinner when Bobby came into the dining room, sat down where she had just laid a placemat, and took her hand in his.

"Muffin, like I told you last night, we've got to set Wolfie back into his natural environment. He's fully grown now, and needs to join a pack or find a mate. It's not fair to keep him from the life he was intended to live."

Meredith withdrew her hand and continued to set out placemats. She had been expecting this conversation but didn't want her step-father to see the painful effect of his words. She knew he was right. She had noticed how Wolfie would leave her bed at night and sit looking through the glass door making simpering sounds until she got up and let him out. Then he would sit on the deck howling—in earnest, not just puppy play. In the last few weeks he had left the deck and disappeared into the bush until dawn. It was time to let him go.

"Won't other wolves kill him?" She asked Bobby.

"That could happen, but he's strong and smart. I think he'll prove worthy."

"So you think they will accept him into the pack?"

"After they're sure he understands that he's not the alpha wolf."

"Not yet, anyway, but I think he will be one day."

"You may be right, Muffin."

Wolfie was strong and smart, a beautiful specimen of a wolf. The high protein content of his lodge diet rendered his agouti coat luxuriously ticked and full. He had clear amber eyes and hard white teeth that glistened in the night. His sense of smell was so acute he could detect fish twenty feet below the surface. He could hear Tom's traps snap at least a mile away in the wilderness.

To prepare Wolfie for his new life, the family made him stay outdoors. There was a lot of pitiful whining at first, Wolfie on one side of the glass door, Meredith on the other. The guides and guests were asked not to pay any attention to him—no petting, no feeding, no baby- or pet-talking to him. Most of them cooperated once they understood the purpose. Outdoors the wolf continued to follow his companion around. Inside the lodge Meredith endured the intense pain of separation from her beloved pet. She tried to act strong, hiding her tears from her mother and especially from Bobby. At night in the dark she would picture wolf fights. She imagined Wolfie attacked, bitten, and bleeding. It was all she could do to keep from getting up, going out onto the deck, flinging her arms around the furry neck, and ushering the wolf back to her bedroom.

In discussions with Bobby, Meredith agreed that Wolfie should be flown farther north and released into the wild at a distance impossible for him to find his way back to Baldwin. They put their heads together over maps of northeastern Manitoba. Bobby explained that it would be best to find an area where there were no commercial lodges or outposts that might lure Wolfie back to his civilized lifestyle. The perfect spot was chosen for the wolf's re-entry into the wild and the date set, weather permitting: July 1st.

Karen said her tearful goodbyes to Wolfie on the floatplane dock. She would stay behind to run the camp. At Bobby's call, the wolf climbed up the rungs between the struts of the Cessna and jumped into his regular seat in the back. Meredith decided to sit in the front with Bobby.

"I can watch what you do and learn how to take off," she told him, although what she really wanted was to crawl into the back, put her arms around the wolf's shoulders, pose her head against the his chest, and listen for the last time to the beating of his strong, loving heart.

They found the nameless lake chosen from the map, landed and pulled into a cove. All three, the pilot and two passengers slipped into the water. Bobby and Meredith waded to shore. Wolfie dog-paddled. Meredith realized that for Wolfie, it was just another adventure. He bounded about, sniffing everything in sight, ducking in and out of the brush. For Bobby it was the right thing to do. But for her it was the end of the happiest days of her life. The ache would be long to heal.

It was over quickly. While she and Wolfie played fetch, Bobby turned the plane around and got aboard, ready to go. Meredith had time to say only a brief goodbye to her wolf. When he bounded after a long toss, she waded out to the plane as fast as she could. Bobby took off the minute she clicked her seat belt. She kept her eyes closed until she knew the lake was out of sight. Only then could she look back.

* * *

The days that followed Wolfie's return to the wild were as dry and void as Carolina cornfields after the harvest. Meredith spent most of the day sitting in front of the lodge on her rock by the lake. When the boats returned in the late afternoon and the guests gathered in the lodge bar exchanging stories about the day's adventures and catch of trophy northern pike and walleye, Meredith couldn't care less. Normally she was right in the middle, picking up bits of information about which lures were hot, where the fish were schooling, how far to let the line out when trolling, and all sorts of fishing tips that had served to make her the best fisherman on the lake. Even old pros would ask her advice. Now she preferred to cope with the pain in solitude.

Her forlorn manner had not escaped the notice of her mother.

"Sugar Baby, I know you miss Wolfie awfully bad. But staying by yourself all the time is only gonna make things worse." Karen had seen her daughter take many a plate of barely-touched food back to the kitchen. After dinner Meredith was in the habit of circulating among the guides to determine the accuracy of the fish tales she had heard from the guests. Now she wandered aimlessly around the camp, up and down the walkway that led east from the main lodge to all the guest cabins, then up and down the walkway that led west from the main building to the guides' bunkhouse and cabins. Finally she would settle, fully clothed, on her bed in her—and Wolfie's—bedroom.

Nothing could pull her out of her doldrums.

* * *

Bobby found her sitting on her favorite boulder by the lake one night after dinner.

"Muffin, I think we should go ahead with the flying lessons. I don't see the need to wait any longer. You're sixteen, you're old enough to earn your license."

"Really?" Bobby's pronouncement brought on the first smile since Wolfie's departure.

"We'll start tomorrow morning, just after all the guests and guides have headed out for the day. There's a pilot's handbook for the Cessna in the plane. You know a lot already. But get it out and look it over tonight, start learning some of the technical terminology." And off she scampered to the floatplane dock, wild curls bobbing. Bobby let out a sigh of relief—and worry. Relief that Meredith's spirits were up again, and worry about the responsibility of teaching one so young to fly over the wilderness.

* * *

That night Meredith dreamed of flying. Rising up off the water she could see the camp below, main lodge and cabins strung out in a straight line parallel to the hard- surface landing strip. Guests were deplaning from the Big Bear DeHaviland Dasher that brought fishermen from Winnipeg to lodges in the north country. This was great fun and joyous freedom! A bird's eye view of the world, and she was in charge. Meredith turned to her copilot.

"Where shall we go today, Wolfie Boy? Up to see the others in your pack? And your mate? I want to see what she looks like."

Clouds moved in, thin at first, but thickening until the ground was obscured. Then Wolfie was not there anymore. She was alone in the sky.

* * *

The morning dawned fair but cold. Bobby kept his promise, so he and Meredith strapped on their seatbelts and sat in the Cessna.

"Okay, Muffin, let's identify all the controls."

He went through the litany. Meredith knew most of the instruments already. Years of observing Bobby's every move and an evening of memorizing the Pilot's Operating Handbook had her ready and eager to fly.

"You must always do a thorough pre-flight inspection. Of everything. Leave nothing to chance. You have to have a flight plan, and it has to be called in. Usually no problem. Use the tail number ID. If you forget, it's written on the placard right there on the instrument panel. And don't forget the log book, which should be filled in before and after the flight. You should start studying the handbook in earnest when we get back."

Bobby gave her precise instruction. He showed her how to start the engine, how to taxi out to face the wind and judge its speed and direction. He demonstrated the effect of rudders, explained how to counter the natural pull to the left, and reviewed the use of flaps and ailerons.

They taxied out for takeoff.

"You keep the yoke back and the RPMs low to avoid propeller damage. Now put on your headset. Protect your ears."

Meredith did as she was told.

He accelerated and the floats dug into the water. The plane nosed up, seemed to pass over a hump which Bobby called the "step," then planed out, skimming easily over the surface of the water.

"The rest is up to principles of physical aerodynamics. You will get lift sooner or later. Just pay attention to the gauges." Bobby spoke in a loud voice. Still it was hard to hear what he was saying above the noise of the engine, and with her headset on, but Meredith knew enough to fill in the gaps. Once airborne, they circled the lake a few times and landed in the same direction as the take-off, against the wind.

Lessons continued almost daily the rest of the summer. Meredith resumed her normal routine of mingling with the guests, helping her mother, Bobby, the chef, the waitress, and the guides whenever and wherever she could. By the time the bear hunters arrived in late summer, she was sitting in the pilot seat. She knew where all equipment and supplies were stored. She knew how to fly the Cessna.

Bobby's friend Paul, a pilot hired to do all the flying between the lodge and the five outposts and a certified flight instructor, went up with Meredith for the last few lessons. By the end of summer, two weeks before she was to return to Winnipeg and begin the twelfth grade, Meredith did her solo and became a licensed pilot. The whole camp celebrated the event.

That night she lay in bed wide awake. It seemed too good to be true. The deepest desire of her heart ever since she could remember was now a reality. She was a pilot, a bush pilot. She could fly a float plane. She loved Bobby for teaching her, and she loved her mother for marrying him after her father's death. From her bed she could see the sky. Swatches of pale light were appearing and disappearing. As she watched the glowing Northern Lights, she formulated a plan, a plan that thrilled her but also scared her to death.

Chapter Three

As usual Wolfie was excited about another trip in the floatplane. He loved to fly and ran ahead of Meredith and Bobby. With two leaps from the dock he was in his seat in the back of the plane. Meredith would come to sit beside him of course.

Wait. She's sitting in the front with Bobby. Why not back here with me where she always sits? This is strange.

Wolfie stretched his neck forward and stuck his nose toward his mistress. She turned to him, petted his muzzle then busied herself fastening her seatbelt. He gave a short, questioning bark.

"Aren't you going to sit next to me for the ride?" She ignored it. He whined. She ignored that, too.

Bobby climbed in and started the engine. Wolfie's attention shifted to the flight.

This is going to be fun. I bet we're flying to one of the outposts. I'll get to smell lots of new things. But I hope there are no humans there. I just want to be with my family.

None of the fisherhumans have ever hurt me, but I still don't trust them all—like the one that talked to Meredith out by the lake a while back.

Take-off was Wolfie's favorite part of a plane ride. The skimming along the surface and the rise into the air. Wolfie felt like a giant of heaven when he could look down from above onto the earth. The lodge camp became smaller and smaller. But he liked to think he was becoming larger and larger—the biggest wolf in the world. He glanced at Meredith, to see if she were having fun like him. But, no, she seemed sad, as though something bad had happened, or was going to happen.

He stood up on the seat and poked his head in front of his mistress.

"It's okay, Wolfie. We're going to find you a new home where you can live the life of a real wolf. It'll be wonderful for you. You will be so happy in the wilderness."

She's trying to tell me something I don't want to hear or understand. Both Meredith and Bobby seem so distant, so cold toward me. She's sitting in the front. Not in the back with her arm around me the way she always does. What's going on?

Pushing aside his quandary, Wolfie continued to enjoy the view of treetops and lakes—so many of them. Every now and then he would put his muzzle on Meredith's shoulder, checking to see if her mood had improved. She would pat his head but did not turn around to face him.

This is a long flight, too far for one of the outposts. I wonder where we're going?

After a while Wolfie grew tired of watching the scene below and settled down in the seat with his chin on his paws. He positioned his head where he could see his mistress. He was just dozing off when he felt the plane bank for landing. He liked this part, too. He felt as though he were a wolf with wings gliding earthward. He saw the water coming closer and closer.

When the floats touched down, he watched the trees along the shoreline fly by so fast.

This isn't one of the outposts. A new lake Bobby is investigating? Why take me and Meredith with him? Why no fishing equipment? This is different. And it confuses me. I'll just have to wait and see what they do here.

Meredith turned around and ruffled the fur behind Wolfie's ears. That calmed his misgivings.

Bobby slipped out of the cockpit and into the water, grabbed the mooring ropes and secured the plane.

"Come on, Wolfie boy, let's go play!"

Finally Meredith was paying real attention to him.

"Okay, you lead the way and I'll follow," Wolfie yipped as he maneuvered his way down the struts after his mistress. *Getting out of the plane sure is harder than getting in.*

After a few strokes in the water, his paws touched the bottom, and he was out on the shore. He vigorously shook the excess moisture from his fur.

Meredith found a stick and threw it. Wolfie ran after it, grabbed it in his teeth, ran a little farther, then crouched on his belly and began to chew.

I know she wants me to bring it back to her, but I want to chomp on it for a while. My teeth need to dig into something hard.

Meredith came up, took the stick away, and threw it again. The sandy shore was perfect for this game. After a few more throws, Meredith knelt beside him, put her arms around his neck, and leaned her head against his.

This doesn't seem to be a game. She's crying. And we were having such a good time. What is wrong?

Wolfie put aside his questions and gave in to the warmth of affection coming from this being he cherished more than anything.

"I love you, Wolfie. I will always love you. And I will never forget you."

Wolfie didn't try to interpret what she said. Whatever it was, it was both beautiful and unsettling to him. He just did not understand. He didn't want to understand. He was relishing the feel of her hand caressing his fur and the gentle sound of her voice filling his heart. Someday soon he would open his inner ears to learn exactly what she was saying to him. But not now. Not yet.

"One last time," Meredith picked up the gnawed-on stick and tossed it long and hard. Wolfie took off after it.

I'll be good this time and bring it back to her.

* * *

Why is the floatplane gliding away from me? Where are they going—without me? Wolfie was bewildered. They never left him behind like this. Meredith had romped with him on the shore, given him rocks and sticks to sniff and inspect. She sat with him and caressed his neck and ears. She spoke to him in her gentle, loving voice. They were having so much fun. Then she rushed back to the plane, Bobby was already in the cockpit. The engine started, and the plane moved away from the bank, away from him. He stood there, barking with urgency.

"Wait! Wait! You've forgotten me!" But they didn't wait. He splashed into the water and tried to swim after them, but the plane moved faster than his paws. He paddled back to shore, shook out his dense fur again, and watched the sky. He could hear the sound of the engine, but Bobby had taxied out of sight. Wait. As always, the plane would taxi toward one end of the lake, turn around, then gather momentum before it would rise and disappear into the clouds. He had seen it day after day at home.

The chugging of the engine grew fainter as it moved farther away. In a few seconds he heard the engine accelerating. Then the plane roared past in rapid ascent and vanished into the sky.

"They'll come back for me. I'd better stay put right here."

So Wolfie sat on a large flat rock at the end of a strip of shoreline that jutted into the water. He sat for a long time, turning his ears like semaphores, capturing sound in all directions. As the sun approached the horizon, the air cooled. Wolfie stretched his front paws out and lowered his belly to the surface of the rock to absorb its stored warmth. Still listening, still looking, he rested his chin on his paws. Occasionally he would lift his head, sure that he heard a distant hum, the return of the plane. Evening insects buzzed his ears. Pine needles hissed in the light breeze. A passing turtle lifted his lazy eyelids, gave the wolf a reptilian glance, and swam on. Once the sun disappeared below the horizon, instinct propelled Wolfie to leave the peninsula and continue his vigil in a less vulnerable spot. He retreated to the covering of the bushes along the shore. He sat. He lay down. He waited. The western sky displayed striated bands of purple, pink, blue, and orange that blazed for a while and faded. A hazy darkness settled over the lake.

The floatplane never flies at night. At that thought Wolfie began to whimper like the little lost, abandoned puppy he once was. *She will find me again, just like she did before.* He whined himself to sleep.

A sound pierced the nocturnal silence, waking Wolfie from pleasant dreams of sitting in the boat with Meredith, running along the lake shore beside her, and keeping watch by her bed. It took him a moment to realize where he was and remember his circumstances, his abandonment and fear. He turned his head toward the forest and listened. There it was again. A mourning sound not unlike the loons of his home lake, only stronger and longer. A song of the wild heart sung in chorus. As he listened to the rising and falling pitches, powerful urges began to ebb and flow with them in his breast. Nighttime impulses were not unknown to Wolfie. He had felt them even as he lay beside Meredith's bed, and he became restless, driven to go outside. When Meredith opened the door to let him out, natural desires intensified. Tonight the wailing sounds were so close, so forceful upon his lupine spirit, that he couldn't help but yield himself. He sat up, lifted his muzzle high, closed his eyes, and howled as he had never howled before.

He chanted the ancient song until the other wolves fell silent, satisfied with their declarations. His instincts were now in control, dictating a course of action: he would sleep for a while, then, at first light, he would find his brothers.

* * *

Wolfie awoke hungry. *Where is Meredith with my food?* He sniffed. Faint odors of airplane fuel and metal still hung in the morning air, reminding him of home. He scanned the lake and sky one last time for any signs of his human family, waiting, listening. He inhaled the faint traces of them lingering on the shore. Then he turned and slipped into the bush, into his ancestral home.

The boreal forest was full of wonders to the wolf's nose and ears. Some he recognized, others were unknown and exotic to him. At first hesitant to roam through the thick underbrush, he soon lost all reservation and began to delight in the richness of the smells and sounds around him. Something deep inside him awakened and responded to it all—the flicking of birds scratching among leaves on the forest floor, the fluttering of wings on the limb of a poplar tree, the distant bellow of a bull moose, and the raucous cry of Canada geese. The stringent tang of chickadees mingled with the cool sweetness of pines. The rich, warm fragrance of a lynx countered the pungent odor of a black bear. The wind off the lake, filtering through the dense greenery, set whiffs of fish and waterfowl adrift in the air.

He picked up a scent that made him salivate. He'd smelled it before, but never paid any attention to it. This was something he could eat. And he was hungry. Eat. Follow the aroma. He held his nose up and followed. As the smell grew stronger, Wolfie knew he was getting close to his prey. He lowered his body and moved more stealthily, drawing in deep, quiet breaths. Something moved in a bush a few meters in front of him. He stopped dead still and waited. Instinct and his nose told him this was the creature he had been stalking. After a while it hopped out of the bush. Wolfie recognized the two long vertical ears of a snowshoe hare. In an instant the nape of the rabbit's neck was between his jaws, and Wolfie was running full speed.

Where to? Where can I eat it and be safe? Wolfie slowed his pace, came to a halt, and sat on his haunches. Before releasing his hold on the struggling rabbit, he clenched his teeth tighter. His fangs went deeper into the flesh of the rabbit's neck and severed the lifeline. The rabbit fell in a limp heap in front of the wolf. Raising his head to make sure he was alone before devouring his first kill, Wolfie found himself looking directly into the eyes of one of his kind.

He pulled back his lips and bared his teeth. A low growl rose in his throat. Head lowered, he stared at the other wolf. Neither moved. During the face-off Wolfie noticed the frailty of his opponent. Rib bones were showing, fur was thin and patches were missing.

I can fight this wolf. I'm bigger. I'm stronger.

He cautiously bent his back legs in preparation to spring, knowing the other wolf would do the same. But his adversary did the unexpected. In an act of submission, it dropped its belly to the ground then rolled on its back, exposing sagging teats. Wolfie, still crouching, inched forward then stood fully erect over the passive female. He lowered his head and sniffed. Her aroma filled his nostrils. He had never smelled a female wolf. His stomach fluttered, his whole body trembled, flooded by strange sensations.

"Who are you?" he demanded.

"I am no one," she stammered.

"Why are you no one?"

She rolled back onto her belly and lifted her head. "I have no pack. My mate, the alpha, was shot by a hunter."

"And . . .?"

"And the new alpha female convinced them all that I should be made to leave the pack . . . with my pups."

That explains the appearance of her belly. "Where are they?"

"Please. If you kill them, kill me, too!"

"I kill only to eat. I was just about to eat this rabbit."

"Yes, I know. I saw you take it and followed you, hoping you would not eat it all." She pushed up to a sitting position.

"You're hungry, then. And your pups, too."

"Yes. They're starving."

Her words summoned up a distant past for Wolfie. He turned, retrieved the rabbit, and dropped it in front of the female.

"Eat. Eat it all. I'll find another for your pups."

"Why are you helping me?"

"Someone once helped me."

The female stood up, took the rabbit in her teeth, and turned to go. Wolfie could see how emaciated she was. As she walked away, he noticed her limping.

"Wait!" he called.

She stopped and turned her head back toward him, the rabbit hanging from her maw. Wolfie could see sorrow and defeat in her eyes.

"I'll go with you. So I will know where to bring the food."

Without another word, she continued her way, and Wolfie followed. She plodded slowly and cautiously through the forest, pausing every now and then to listen. To what Wolfie didn't know. He heard nothing except the hiss of the wind in the pines. *I have much to learn,* Wolfie realized.

They reached a tangled clump of fallen poplar and pine limbs under which she had dug out a cave to form a den. Two ragged pups crawled out to meet her. When they saw Wolfie they bared their young fangs and hissed. They were frightened, and they were starving, but they were brave. Wolfie watched the mother quickly devour the rabbit then regurgitate it in front of the pups. They tore into the warm meal and soon forgot about the presence of a large male.

While the pups ate, Wolfie turned to the mother.

"Why are their eyes blue?"

"Have you never seen young ones before?"

"Well . . .no, I haven't."

"They all have blue eyes when they come forth from the mother. But they will be changing soon. In fact, the male pup already has one golden eye."

"What are their names, and how old are they?"

"They are Nuba and Arn. Two moons old," the mother said.

"And what is your name?"

She arched her neck, looked squarely into his amber eyes for the first time, and answered, "I am Patanya, alpha female of the White Moon Pack. Or *was*." She dropped her gaze.

Wolfie could detect vestiges of her former dignity despite her sad state. There was something regal about her bearing. She was proud and humble at the same time. She did without food so the pups could eat. As bony as she was, she radiated beauty. All this amazed and confounded Wolfie.

"And you?" she asked.

"My name is Maengun."

He didn't know why he spoke his original Ojibwe name. It had almost never been used, not for a long time. But for some reason it came out when she asked. His old name had become his new name. It seemed right.

"I was raised by humans and was part of their pack. They have pushed me away, too. Like you. I need to learn the ways of the forest. Will you help me? I will protect you and the pups. I will be your male."

She turned her sad eyes on him. "I will help you. I will be your female."

Maengun trotted up to Patanya, gently took the scruff of her neck in his mouth, and held it for a few seconds. Then, releasing his hold, he dropped his muzzle toward hers. He closed his eyes while her soft tongue licked his face. The regular rhythm of the strokes mesmerized him and filled him with peace. He could sense her relief and gratitude. Or was it his own?

* * *

Hunting was not easy. Maengun realized now that he had been lucky with that first rabbit. He had been unsuccessful in the next few attempts—two red squirrels and another rabbit had gotten away.

"Squirrels are impossible! They can disappear up a tree so fast, then they sit up there, twitching their fluffy tails and mocking me with that *chucking* sound they make. I'd like to catch one just to show them." He was crouched on his belly expressing himself to one of the rodent rascals perched on the lowest limb of a white pine, just out of reach, making that revolting chiding noise at him.

"Shut up! If I really wanted to eat you, you'd be in my stomach right now. But you scrawny things don't have much meat on your bones. Besides you're not very tasty, you know." Maengun lowered his head and thought of Patanya and the pups. He must bring them something.

A flash of silver. In his peripheral vision Maengun saw something move between the tree trunks to his left. The hackles came up.

What was that? Too small for a bear, too big for rabbit. Silver yet dark. What else could it be but a wolf?

He stood on all fours and listened. Not a sound. Nothing moving. He waited several minutes. Then he sensed a movement to his right. He had to turn his head only slightly to spot a lynx ducking through the brush. He lowered his body almost to the ground, locking his vision on the cat. As the prey moved, so did Maengun. When the cat stopped, so did the wolf.

This will not be easy. There should be at least two of us, one to attack from the front, one from the rear.

A silver shadow flickered among the trees just beyond the lynx. Maengun sharpened his vision. Something was there, ahead, stalking the prey with him. He thought he saw two golden eyes glowing like embers in the shadows, but he couldn't be sure. The cat must have sensed danger, for he slowly turned in a circle, looking in all directions around him. Maengun knew the animal was about to make a run for it, so he tensed his shoulder muscles and crouched into springing position.

When he moves again, I will attack.

It all happened fast. The lynx leapt forward and Maengun lunged. The cat was fast, faster than Maengun had presumed. Nevertheless he went in pursuit at full speed, chasing him over logs, underneath bushes, and between trees. The cat was nimble, and despite his powerful lope, the wolf was losing ground. There was a fierce snarl, the cat's front paws buckled and he fell on his side, kicking with all fours. A large silver and black wolf had a death grip on the cat's throat and had pulled him down. Maengun rushed forward and took a rear flank in his jaws. Ferocious growls came forcefully from his throat as he fought to help subdue the struggling prey. Both wolves held tenaciously until the lynx lay lifeless. Maengun plunged his teeth into the cat's belly and tore into the warm entrails. He gulped down several large bites before he remembered the mysterious wolf that had actually made the kill. He lifted his head, expecting to find his partner feasting beside him. But there was no one, nothing. Maengun was alone. He looked around him straining to see through the dense forest.

Still breathing fast from the high-speed chase and the thrill of victory over his prey, Maengun yelped in short gasps. "Who are you? Where did you come from? Where did you go?"

No response. The other wolf had vanished as quickly as he had appeared. Why did he not eat? Maengun waited to see if the strange wolf would reappear. He glanced over his right shoulder then the left. But there was no sign of the silver and black wolf. Maengun continue to eat. Once he had filled his stomach, his pulse resumed its normal rate and his head cleared. He remembered the female and her hungry pups.

I must either get this food to them or bring them to it. If I leave it here the other wolf or some other meat-eater will probably devour it.

He set his incisors and fangs into the cat's rear flank and tore off a leg. He carried it to the base of a nearby poplar and, digging furiously, buried it. He did the same with the other flank. He grabbed the nape of the lynx's neck and, empowered by determination to fulfill his promise, began to drag the remainder of the carcass over the forest floor.

If I encounter the silver and black wolf again, I will share the meat. It is rightfully his more than mine.

Pausing only twice to rest, he found his way back to Patanya's den with the meal. The pups bounded to meet him, yipping excitedly before wildly setting their teeth into the fresh kill, trying their best to eat like grown wolves.

Patanya remained lying by the entrance to the den. Maengun nosed her forehead, rubbed his muzzle against hers, then dropped to his belly to lie beside her and watch the pups nipping at the carcass and learning to eat on their own.

"It looks like the pups are eating for themselves now."

"They are making an effort, although they still prefer to let us do the work for them." She sat up to watch the young ones.

"There's more than enough for you, too, Patanya."

"Yes, I see. You are quite a hunter to take down an adult lynx by yourself."

"I didn't." Although he would have enjoyed his mate's admiration, Maengun decided to be honest.

"What do you mean?"

"Another wolf appeared out of the forest—like a shadow—and brought the lynx down. I helped a little. Then he just disappeared completely, without eating."

"Was he black and silver?"

"Yes, how did you know?"

"It was Ganu, my alpha mate."

"But isn't he dead? You said that hunters shot him."

"It is his spirit. I have seen it, too. He has helped me more than once. One day when he was still the alpha he told me that he would always watch over me, even after death." She dropped her head for a moment, then lifted it, looking directly into Maengun's bright yellow eyes. "He has accepted you as my new male. Otherwise he would not have helped you."

Maengun hesitated to reply. "I must think about all this. It's confusing to me. I'm afraid I don't understand."

"It is the way of the wilderness, not of your human world. You asked me to teach you. Now you are learning." Patanya raised herself to all fours. "The pups are not quite ready to eat directly. Keep watch while I eat to feed them."

Maengun admired her regal bearing as she trotted toward the carcass. Ganu had taught him an invaluable lesson: wolves were not meant to hunt alone. They are brothers and the pack is their strength and their identity.

"Wait, Patanya." Maengun rose and followed her. "Feed yourself. I have eaten too much. Let me feed Nuba and Arn. And from the contents of his stomach Wolfie released the pups' meal.

Chapter Four

For the next few light cycles Maengun became Patanya's pupil. He hoped he wasn't annoying her with all his questions. He wanted to know the best time and place to hunt different food sources. He was particularly eager to learn how to outsmart a squirrel. She knew so much about the ways of the wilderness, and Meangun drank it all in. He spent long hours wandering about the bush watching and listening to the forest creatures. He especially liked the birds. They made pleasant little chirping, chukking, and whistling sounds that fascinated him. He wished he had wings to flap and fly like they do. He imagined it would be fun to live in the trees, hopping from branch to branch. However, a diet of seeds and berries didn't appeal to him at all. Most of the winged creatures paid no attention to him—except the crows. Sometimes a crow would follow him, swooping through the trees, lighting here and there to watch him.

One morning when the warmth of the sun was caressing the earth and waters, Maengun woke up with a touch of wanderlust. He stretched himself—front end low with paws forward and back end up—a kind of bow to the great light—and went to look for his mate. As usual Patanya was already busy washing the pups ears, her tongue moving in regular rhythmic patterns.

"I think I'll go exploring. Want to come with me?"

"You go ahead. There are some hunting lessons I want to teach these two today."

After rubbing muzzles with his family, Maengun set out with his blood crying for adventure and his stomach calling for food. He had been on the prowl only a short time when a shadow grazed his vision. Then he heard the noisy flapping of large wings. Glancing up he saw a crow settling on the branch of a jack pine, bobbing his tail to keep his balance.

"Why are you following me?" Maengun uttered a throaty rumble, displaying his aggravation at being tracked.

The crow gave no response, but cocked his head a bit then let out a raucous scream that Maengun couldn't understand.

"You don't have a very pretty voice, bird. What do you want from me?"

Still nothing from the black pest.

In spite of his irritation, Maengun couldn't help but admire the crow's feathers so shiny black that they reflected iridescent hues of pink, blue, and gold.

"I'll have to ask Patanya about this. She'll explain why the crow hangs around me." He articulated the statement aloud in yips and barks, hoping that the crow would understand. *I wonder if crows can understand wolves? I certainly can't understand that awful noise they make.*

Maengun's quandary about the crows was interrupted by loud squawking coming from the direction of the lake. He loped away to investigate. Peering through the foliage at the water's edge he witnessed a monumental standoff between two loons. With their chests puffed out and wings flapping, they stood upright on the water and seemed to be dancing, a dance of defiance.

One of them must be defending his territory, Maengun surmised.

"Look along the shoreline," an inner voice said.

Maengun dropped his head and let his eyes sweep over the water's edge. Slightly elevated above the water line and partially hidden by a chokecherry bush, he spotted a nest. A nest with two loon chicks. He could see the little furry things standing up, with their beaks open. He could smell their warm, sweet aroma.

They are small, but I bet they are tender and juicy. I bet the pups could eat one of these.

Without any further thinking, Maengun lowered his body and slipped out of the bush. A few seconds was all it took to fill his mouth with one of the chicks. The adult loons were still arguing and bobbing around on the water. Maengun knew he would have no problem getting away unnoticed . . . until his crow friend started cawing at the top of his lungs.

He's wasting his breath trying to warn the loons, if that's what he's doing.

Maengun threaded his way through tree trunks, bushes, and underbrush, distancing himself as quickly as possible from the loons.

They are so involved in their dispute, the parents won't notice the missing chick for a while. By then it will be in my belly.

Maengun found a little enclosure—a patch of moss surrounded by tall bushes where he felt safe to eat his freshly acquired lunch. No one around except the crow, sitting high above him. One gulp was all it took. It wasn't nearly enough. He longed for a more substantial meal. He dropped to his belly on the soft moss and, licking his lips, began to review the questions he would ask Patanya when he got back to the den.

Why does a crow follow me through the woods?

How do loons puff up and dance around on top of the water? Why do they do that?

How soon can the pups start eating on their own instead of depending on us to eat it first?

But the one question uppermost in his mind he would not ask her: *How can I kill an animal large enough to feed all four of us for a while? How can I do this without help?*

Maengun felt ashamed of eating the bite-sized loon chick originally intended for the pups. But he knew the small meals of rabbits and martens that he had been able to provide his family were inadequate. He longed for greater exploits. There was still so much he had to learn about being a wolf in the wild. But with each light cycle his new life was becoming more natural. Although his questions were fewer now, the wilderness was ever full of surprises.

* * *

Maengun dropped a squirrel in front of Patanya. Standing in front of her with pride for this first squirrel, he watched as she ate the meal and regurgitated food for the pups. He relished the joy he was beginning to feel as a hunter, as a provider, and realized that it came to him from the gratitude he saw in Patanya's golden eyes. At first light he had seized two rabbits and now this red squirrel—all of which he had caught by himself with no help from the silver shadow. It was enough food to satisfy his new family for a while, although he himself was still hungry. No matter. The rush of the chase, the thrill of the capture—that was sustaining him now. He was doing what his bones and blood dictated. His wild instincts were in charge of his thoughts, feelings, and actions. For the first time, he was aware of his sharp fangs, how they could sink into flesh and fill his mouth with the taste of blood, the power they had over life and death. His thick fur protected him from briars, nettles, and sharp twigs. The agouti coloration with its bands of black, white, gray, gold, and brown was an effective camouflage that hid him in the brush and kept him from being detected by his prey and also kept him from being prey to any bear on the prowl. He was becoming a skillful wolf. He had a mate and pups. He could hunt and kill. But there was something lacking, something profound, that needed satisfying more than hunger. That night he discovered what it was.

Lying in the semi-darkness of the northern night just outside the den where Patanya, Arn, and Nuba slept, he inhaled the aromas of the forest. He saw the gleam of light refracted in the eyes of small creatures foraging cautiously in the night. He could hear the regular breathing of the sleeping female and young. At last, what he had been waiting for, the howling. He rose to all fours and listened intently. One wolf, then two, then more joined in, calling to one another with undulating pitches, a haunting sound that penetrated deep into his primeval nature. The sound of the pack. No doubt the same pack that ousted Patanya and her pups. Stronger than his urge to howl, more powerful than his need to hunt, to eat, or to mate, was this compelling force to be part of a pack. To stalk an animal larger than himself, a hooved animal, follow it, then attack it with his brothers, tear at it together until they could bring it down and share its meat. Only then could he take pride in his wolfness, only then would he be a true wolf. He lifted his muzzle, closed his eyes, and let his spirit cry out.

"Here-------I am-------. Here-------I am----------Here-------I am!"

A lone wolf responded, "Who are you? Where are you?" in long, wailing wolf cries.

Maengun repeated his location message.

He paused in his howling to hear a compelling voice coming to him from his own heart. He listened and he understood. In the next light cycle he would find them, and of one thing he was now sure—he was destined to lead them. Maengun shook himself. Become the alpha wolf of a pack he had never been part of? Had he let his imagination run wild? Maybe that was okay. After all, he was in the wild now, he had returned to his heritage, and he had a wilderness family. He thought about it for a moment. No, it wasn't imagination—that is a human trait, one he must shed. It was instinct, a sense deep within, a sense that had now become the ruling order of his life. It would direct his life. It would save his life and that of other wolves.

The late summer night was cool, the air thinner. He could smell better through the chill. His nose detected Patanya. He thought he recognized the aroma of warm blood coursing in her neck.

"She and the pups are vulnerable when they sleep. I need to be with them. I need to be more vigilant."

With a sense of urgency plaguing his mind, Maengun ducked back into the den and squirmed between the logs to get inside. The three wolves lay in a heap, one pup draped over the mother's middle, another curled up under her chin.

There was barely enough room for the three of them, much less another adult. Maengun had to inch his way low to the ground to get his nose next to Patanya's muzzle. One of the pups stirred in his sleep, letting out a soft moan before settling down again. The smell of the female wolf and pups was powerful in the den and Maengun drank it in with each breath. He licked his mate's face and lightly nipped her ears. She partially opened her eyes then closed them again, peacefully receiving the gentle affection of her male.

"I will lie outside at the entrance and keep watch," he whispered to the three sleeping wolves. Turning himself to exit the den required skill and flexibility. Once his head was outside Maengun filled his lungs with the fresh night air. He stood for a while and listened. Then he sat, cocking his head first one way then the other.

"All is well," he assured himself and lay with front legs stretched out in front of him. He propped his chin over his forearms, but his eyes remained wide and his ears alert to the least sound of the forest. He thought of his plans to find the pack and tried to imagine what would happen when he did. His heart began to pound. *What if they kill me? What will become of Patanya and the pups?* As he visualized fighting for his life and that of his family, his blood rose, his nostrils flared, and his pelt trembled with excitement. He closed his eyes and focused on the voice of the wilderness in his heart of hearts. Again it told him to go, to fight, to lead the pack. "I can—and I will."

When he opened his eyes light was filling the forest.

* * *

Maengun was waiting for Patanya when she squirmed out of the den. He licked her muzzle and ears then sat on his haunches in front of her.

"What? What do you need to tell me?" she asked.

"I'm going to find the pack. You can join me if you like, with the young ones."

"Why? Why are you going?"

"I have to."

"Why do you have to? We're all right here, as we are."

"If we are to survive, we need the pack. You know that as well as I."

Patanya dropped her head in deference to her mate.

"Then go if you must. I'll stay here. They don't want me."

"They will."

He nuzzled to reassure her. He had known she would not sanction this endeavor, one he himself was not eager to embark on. Maengun wondered if his nighttime illuminations were real. He wondered if he shouldn't stay with his mate and leave well-enough alone. Yet he had to find out. It would be hard to turn away from his female. It would be so much simpler to stay with her and the young ones. He and Patanya could provide for the cubs, just the two of them. He could be facing his own death, then his family would have little or no chance of survival. But something compelled him. He must find the others wolves. Though he was new to the wilderness, the wilderness was not new to him, it was in his veins, it permeated his being.

A sudden wind swept past his nostrils, bringing to his olfactory sense all the powerful aromas of the forest. An intoxicating blend of evergreens—cedar, juniper, pine, spruce. The alluring smell of prey—beaver, rabbit, moose, even the faint but irresistible scent of caribou. Something, a force as old as Nature itself, stirred the core of his being. His pupils widened, the flesh of his shoulders quivered. Closing his inward ears to the voice of his mind, he listened to a deeper summons, turned away from his mate, and headed into the bush.

* * *

Maengun could hear the rush of a waterfall. He was thirsty and knew he could drink at the stream flowing from it, so he headed toward the sound. When he neared the water he stopped short, keeping himself hidden in the brush. From where he stood he could smell a large beast. His pupils widened, his nostrils flared. He eased forward, quietly parting the greenery with his muzzle. In the midst of the stream a magnificent moose foraged, his head underwater. Maengun's muscles contracted and he crouched into a springing position. Suddenly the moose lifted his head. Water dripped from his enormous rack and from the flap of his chin bell.

The wolf's blood stirred. His heart beat faster. *He knows I'm here,* Maengun sensed. He saw a flash of fear in the dark eyes, but the moose didn't flinch. The wolf began to salivate. Neither of the two moved for a moment.

From somewhere inside him an ancestral voice counseled. *You can't do this alone. You need the pack.* With this realization, the wolf's muscles relaxed and without a sound he slipped out of the brush, turning away from his would-be prey. Heading downstream he slaked his thirst with the cold, clear water, glided back into the forest, and continued the search for his brothers.

He found a trail rife with a variety of animal odors. He recognized some—wolf, bear, rabbit, marten, squirrel, and fox. But there was another that startled him. *Human.* An image of Meredith surged in his inner vision. He sat on his haunches, closed his eyes, lifted his muzzle, and sniffed. *Male human.* The inner voice warned him of danger. *No, this human—these humans—are different. They are to be feared. They come to take life from the animals. You must beware of them.* He proceeded with due caution, all his senses alert.

An ear-splitting *crack* sent him bounding into thick covering. Human voices were yelling to each other. Maengun stayed hidden. He could hear the men shuffling about in the bush not far ahead. Then he detected the odor of blood, the blood of a large animal. The blood of a bear. Despite his fear, he started salivating again. He needed meat.

I am hungry, but I must wait. These humans have taken the life of a bear. They could take mine.

He waited. The crunch of footsteps. From his hiding place he could see the humans moving along the trail. They carried rifles and a small bundle. Maengun's nose told him there were bear parts in the bundle. His instincts told him to wait. He waited a long time until he could no longer hear their steps, until he could hear a distant boat motor revving, until his inner voice told him it was safe to come out of hiding.

He crept close to the ground toward the trail, pausing in the underbrush to look and listen on all sides every few meters. Satisfied that he was safe, he continued his journey, loping along the path until he came upon the body of the mutilated bear. He walked around it, curious and hungry. Its belly had been cut open, some inner parts removed, and his paws had been severed.

The humans have taken what they wanted. Now I can eat. He approached the carcass and sank his teeth into the fat of the open belly. Instantly he felt sharp pain in his shoulder. Another set of teeth was set in his own flesh. He turned to find himself surrounded by bared fangs and snarling muzzles. He shook off his attacker and backed away from the dead bear. Instinctively he lifted his lips in a snarl. A fierce, threatening growl rose from his throat. The hair on his neck bristled. On all sides hostile amber eyes glared at him.

I must either lie down in submission or be prepared to fight them all. No, I will not submit. Maengun stood tall and spoke:

"Brothers, I have not come to fight you. I have come to lead you." None of them moved. He spoke again: "I am strong, and I am fearless. It is my destiny to lead this pack."

One wolf backed away, still growling and keeping his lips raised. A second followed suite. A third, and a fourth. Although they had distanced themselves, Maengun was surrounded by menacing strangers. Only one remained close, facing Maengun in an adversarial stance. The alpha. The lead wolf began to circle his opponent. Maengun turned in place, his eyes locked on those of the other wolf. The pack wolf sprang, head low, going for the throat. Maengun lowered his shoulders so that the bite missed the throat but caught his cheek. The two wolves reared up on hind legs, the pack wolf holding his clench on Maengun's muzzle, both wolves snarling and foaming at the mouth. Maengun managed to dig his fangs in the alpha's lip, causing him to drop his hold.

They lunged at each other again and again, rising and falling, rolling over one another, each trying to avoid the deadly fangs of the other. Maengun fought hard. Ignoring his bleeding cheek and shoulder, he reared up against his opponent. The pack wolf met him face on and caught Maengun's wounded cheek in his teeth once again. Maengun felt the sharp pain. But he was the larger and more powerful wolf. The heavier weight of his body caused his adversary to lose his balance. The smaller wolf relaxed his jaws as he fell. Maengun pounced and set a death grip in the nape of the alpha's neck. He stood over his conquest, a low growl churning in his throat. When he was satisfied that the other wolf was subdued, he released his hold.

"You are weak, brother. You need food. You may eat first."

The defeated wolf lay on his side with his head on the ground for a moment then slowly rose to a lowered stance. He raised his eyes briefly to Maengun before creeping to nourish himself on fresh bear meat. Maengun was next at the carcass. But he couldn't eat. Still keyed up from the battle, he turned away from the meal as if satiated. He took a few steps away, licked the blood from his lips, and stood, head high, waiting to see what would happen. The other wolves ceased their snarling. Maengun could sense their aggression turning to confusion and fear. Hesitant at first, one by one they lowered their heads, crept forward, and began to share in the feast. They ate in silence for a while, each raising a blood-covered muzzle occasionally to glance at Maengun then returning to feed. When all the wolves had eaten their fill and lay nearby cleaning their forepaws, Maengun spoke.

"We must bury the rest of the meat for another meal. Do you have a safe place?"

The defeated wolf looked at the others before answering. "I will show you."

"Then let each of you take a large piece, enough to feed two of us in meager times. We will go together to fill our cache."

Despite their uncertainty at the upheaval of the old order, the wolves did as told, leaving what remained of the bear for forest scavengers. Maengun and the defeated wolf, side by side, led the way. The others in single file followed the old guide and their new alpha wolf to prepare for the future. Drops of blood from Maengun's wounds soaked into the forest floor.

* * *

"Maengun, you're hurt!"

"It's nothing. Where are the young ones?"

"They're in the den, sleeping. What happened to you? You've been gone so long."

"I encountered the pack and had to fight the alpha."

"You fought? Let me see how bad it is." Patanya nosed up to Maengun and began licking his facial wound. "What happened?"

"Everything is okay, Patanya. They have accepted me as their leader. You are now the alpha female—again."

She stopped licking and looked at him in disbelief. "You defeated him?"

"Of course I did. And I told them I had come to lead them."

"And they accepted you?"

"Every one of them."

"I'm really not surprised. You're bigger than any of them, the handsomest wolf I've ever seen. I just hope the females are willing to accept *me*."

"They will. You are Patanya of the White Moon Pack. Next season you will have more pups. Our pups. And the pack will be strong. Now wake the young ones and follow me. Hunters have killed a bear and left most of the meat. The pack has cached a good bit of it. There's plenty of food for everyone."

"How do you know where they have hidden it?"

"I led them there."

"They followed you?"

"The defeated alpha took me to the spot. The others came behind us bringing the meat."

"Then you really are the leader."

"Yes."

Patanya turned and yelped for the pups to come. Maengun could hear the excitement in her call. There was even a hint of joy in her voice for the first time.

He led the mother and her young to the bear carcass. Of course he was happy to have the acceptance of the pack. But he was more pleased over the reinstatement of Patanya as alpha female. It was all happening so fast. The memory of his life among the humans was fading equally as fast. But he was trying hard to cling to one image, one name: *Meredith.* He did not want to let go of that, not yet, not ever.

When they reached the food, some of the wolves had disappeared into the forest. Others were curled up, dozing and digesting. The defeated alpha was the only one fully alert.

"You are doing well to stand guard. What is your name, brother?"

"Naoghi, son of Tabar."

"I'll watch with you, Naoghi, while Patanya and her young ones eat. Then you will take me to the pack gathering place. As the great light drops below the horizon, together we will call to the others and give thanks to the Great Spirit for this meal which came to us without effort on our part. After two light cycles we will hunt . . . as a pack."

During the conversation Naoghi kept his eyes lowered. Despite his defeat, Maengun could detect no resentment from him. Quite the contrary, Naoghi seemed relieved to be free of his leadership position. *He's a good wolf, just not cut out to be an alpha.*

"You could be of great help to me, Naoghi. Can I rely on you?"

"Yes. Always."

Maengun stepped forward and touched his nose to the other wolf's. For an instant their amber eyes met, and Maengun knew he had turned an enemy into an ally.

* * *

When the great light turned red and settled on the horizon, Maengun stood. His blood was surging, his heart wanted to sing. He trotted off toward the glowing sky, found a little hillock, and sat. Lifting his chin he allowed the cry to rise, to express his profound joy, his joy of being a wolf chosen to lead the pack.

"I am Maengun, I am a hunter. I am who and where I was meant to be. I am a wolf in the wild."

"I am Patanya of the White Moon Pack. I am who and where I was meant to be. I am a wolf in the wild."

She had come to sing beside him. So quietly he had not known she was there until she sang. Maengun lowered his muzzle and turned to look at her. With her eyes closed, her head tilted back she sang, her pitches rising and falling grandly, soaring and dipping with conviction. She was obviously more skilled at this than he was. He listened to her for a moment then joined her, their voices combining in a fugal celebration of life.

"Me, too, me ,too."

"Hear me howl, too."

The pups yipped. They had followed their mother to the hillock and now proudly added their high-pitched squeals and barks to the evening song.

Maengun had never experienced this sense of fulfillment. He was happy to bear his responsibilities to his family and to his pack. He had no doubts about his ability. He had no fear of defeat or famine. His pelt trembled with excitement at the prospect of living the full life of his kind. They would hunt together, sing together, play together, sleep together. They would take care of each other. There would be order and obedience. They would survive together.

Chapter Five

The day had been a long one. Not a free moment for Karen to think about the flight to Winnipeg tomorrow. Now, past midnight, she was throwing a few things into a large zip-up bag—a hairbrush and cosmetic case, cell phone, passport for official identification, nightgown, slippers, a change of underwear, extra sweater, and whatever else she hurriedly deemed necessary for the overnight trip.

Assuming the ownership of the lodge on Baldwin Lake had made it difficult for her and Bobby to run five outposts as well as the lodge. They had mutually decided to keep operating Poplar River and Cinnamon Lake outposts, but to relinquish the three others to Ralph, Bobby's longtime friend and fellow outfitter. Tomorrow Bobby would meet with the attorneys, a representative from the provincial government, and Ralph Haygood. New exclusivity contracts had to be drawn and signed. Bobby had rounded up all the relevant financial record books and paperwork and put them in an attaché case which stood ready to go in the office.

They arranged to fly out with Big Bear Airlines after it deposited a party of four guys coming in at midweek for a three-day bear hunt. Tom and Cedrick—the two best—took the job as guides for this group. It was the final week of the season and these hunters were the only ones booked at the lodge. The outposts were closed, awaiting Ralph's upgrades and the long, hard winter ahead.

"'Bout ready for bed, Sweetheart?" Bobby seemed anxious to turn out the light. A long day for him, too.

"Just have to brush my teeth, make my goodnight kiss sweet."

"Mmm. That's sounds inviting."

"Don't get any ideas."

"To be honest, tonight my mind's on business matters."

"You don't anticipate a problem, do you?" Karen asked with a mouthful of toothpaste suds.

"Not with the contract, I'm just concerned about both of us being away from the lodge while there are guests here."

"So am I. But I do need some new jeans and things. Besides, staying at a hotel will be a romantic get-away. Certainly more practical than staying in the house with all the utilities cut off for the summer." She took a swallow of water, rinsed her mouth, wiped it on a towel, and hung the towel back on the rack. Grinning into the mirror, she checked the whiteness of her teeth. *I really will be needing new pants and some loose tops*, she mentally projected to her reflected image.

"Yeah, I guess it has been a while since you've touched base with civilization. I'm sure Tom and Cedrick know how to handle things in the bush."

Karen slid into bed, gave Bobby a kiss on the temple, ran her hand over his dark curls, and nestled into her pillow.

"And Meredith knows how to handle things at the lodge," she yawned.

"I don't like leaving her behind, with that kind of responsibility. I'm surprised she didn't want to come along."

"I'm not surprised that a teenaged tomboy is bored by legal matters and shopping sprees." And so was Karen. She loved her summers in the wilderness and would much rather have stayed at the lodge with Meredith . . . or gone on the bear hunt with Tom . . . or played the electronic keyboard in the lodge apartment . . . or spent the day fishing . . . or . . . but she had to see a doctor.

* * *

Meredith gave Karen and Bobby goodbye hugs just before they ascended the retractable steps of Big Bear's DeHavilland Dasher.

"Have fun—and don't worry!" Meredith said, putting on her best reassuring look of confidence. Her mother had not ceased to proffer all sorts of last minute instructions and cautions to the teen. Meredith knew that Karen had inherited the worry habit from her mother. Probably genetic. She would have to guard against it.

"You're beginning to sound like Granny Kingsley, Mama." That stopped the flood of troublesome advice and elicited a smile from her mother.

"I'll call you tonight, Sugar." Mama's usual parting words, exclaimed from the top step just before ducking into the Dasher. At least she had finally started abbreviating "Sugar Baby."

It seemed like forever before the plane taxied to the back of the gravel runway, turned around, and sped by on its way to the sky, southward bound. Meredith's heart was racing. Soon she would be in that same sky, northward bound.

She helped the guides load the hunters' duffle bags and rifle cases onto a cart for delivery to their cabin. By now the four men were enjoying an enormous breakfast in the dining room. It was Meredith's job to show them to their cabin afterwards and make sure they had all they needed before they set out two-to-a-boat across the lake with Tom and Cedrick. Then her only duty would be answering the lodge phone, the phone with a recorded message that could be switched on when convenient. She would be back at the lodge tonight long before her mother called.

Once the hunters were dispatched with their guns and guides, Meredith hustled back to the lodge. In the office she called in her flight plan to Air Services at Thompson Regional Airport, located the keys to the Cessna, then reached across the desk and pressed the Message button on the answering machine.

"You have reached Baldwin Lake Lodge and Outposts. The office is temporarily closed. Please leave your name, number, and message at the sound of the tone and we will return your call as soon as possible. The Marstens wish you tight lines and calm winds." Karen's voice. Meredith smiled. She loved her mother's voice, even when it provoked her with copious instructions.

Next on the agenda: find the typological map that Bobby marked when they decided where to leave Wolfie. She opened the desk drawer and started to shuffle through it but, lo and behold, what she wanted was right on top of the pile. She took the map from the drawer and spread it out on top of the desk. Leaning on her elbows with her chin cupped in her hands and her legs straight behind her with one ankle draped over the other, she perused the printed landscape. It was all quite familiar to her. Baldwin Lake was labeled and so were some of the neighboring portage lakes. There near the top of the page was the "X" that Bobby had made the night they planned Wolfie's release into a new life. Wolfie's lake had no name or number, but it was on this map, and so was her wolf. And she was going to find him. She spent some time studying the lay of the land, then carefully rolled the map like a sacred scroll unearthed from an ancient cavern.

Satisfied that all was well, she left the office, slid the keys into her jeans pocket, crossed the dining room, and still clutching the scroll, pushed through the swinging door to the kitchen.

"Bonjour, Merri." Emil, their five-star chef for the last two years, was unloading the dishwasher. "Come to 'elp me?" The tall, muscular Quebecois always wore a chef's *toque* which made him tower over the entire staff. At the moment it was hindering his access to dishes at the back of the racks. The cap and his pronounced French accent delighted the guests and probably made their food taste even better. Now that the camp was about to close down, he was the lone cook, bottle-washer, and waiter. Jennifer, the college student who worked as waitress, sous-chef, and occasional bartender, had already returned to the university.

"Sorry, not today." Meredith found a plate of leftover breakfast biscuits and a few strips of bacon on the counter, pulled the flaky biscuits open and stuffed them with the crisp meat. From the refrigerator she took out what was needed to make two turkey sandwiches. She slipped the bacon biscuits and sandwiches into small plastic bags, took a Diet Coke from the pantry, and exited the kitchen via the back door, through the staff dining/meeting room, and into the owners' quarters. From beneath her bed she drew out a backpack she had prepared the night before with items her mother always instructed her to take along on any trip: an extra sweater and a change of underwear. She unzipped the outer section and pushed the food bags and Coke can in. After a last look around, she swung the backpack over one shoulder, pulled a heavy jacket off the peg behind the door of her closet bedroom, and left the main lodge building by the back door, hurrying toward the path that led to the floatplane dock.

Meredith performed all the required pre-flight safety checks, pumped the floats, and verified the gas supply. Paul, the pilot Bobby employed for the past few years, always kept the plane in top shape. No need to worry about mechanical conditions. Meredith climbed into the pilot's seat. The sound of the engine alerted the camp to her departure. She knew it would, but there was nothing they could do about it. She knew that, too. After performing the usual engine checks, she set the transponder to transmit the code assigned to her by Air Services. Placing the headset over her ears, she taxied out to the widest section of the lake and took off full throttle. With only one person aboard and no cargo, the Cessna rapidly gained momentum and lifted off the water.

* * *

Karen chose a seat next to a window toward the rear of the plane, snapped on her seat belt, and leaned back. Bobby was moving up and down the aisle talking with the departing lodge guests. So many of them were return guests, usually the same week every year. They became a fishing family, and the week at the lodge was a kind of family reunion.

"Thanks for coming again this year, guys. We've got you booked for next year, same time, same cabins, same guides."

"Same fish?" one guest quipped.

"Same ones—but they will have grown a few inches. So, more trophies for you."

Karen smiled. Bobby knew how to deal with these guys. No matter what the circumstances, he could psych them up, make them eager to fish the waters of Baldwin Lake again next year.

When he had finished saying his goodbyes to the guests, he sat down next to Karen.

She reached over, took his hand, and gave it a squeeze.

"You're amazing, Bobby Marsten."

Turning toward her, he pulled on the strap to tighten her seatbelt then clicked his own in place.

"If anybody is amazing around here it's you."

The Big Bear taxied to the far end of the runway, did a slow 180-degree turn, and began its run for take-off. Looking down at the camp Karen remembered the first time she came to Baldwin Lake. Bobby had just taken over the management and was routing all his outposts through the lodge. She and her husband Steve, Bobby's cousin, were heading to the Poplar River outpost as they did every summer. Campers going to the various outposts were shuttled over to them from the lodge in the floatplane. It was the largest lake she had ever seen—the far shore was barely visible from the lodge. While they waited their turn to fly out to Poplar, Bobby gave her and Steve a tour of the main building, including the owner's quarters. How could she have ever known that she would be living there—as Bobby's wife—in the not too distant future? Life is full of twists and turns of fate. And she was facing one now.

"What can I get you to drink? The lone flight attendant was leaning in toward Karen. The pocket of her crisp white shirt was embroidered with the head of a growling bear, the airline logo. "Coffee, tea, milk, or a cola?"

"Coffee with cream, please."

"Would you like a doughnut or muffin?"

"No, thank you. Just coffee."

Maybe the coffee will help settle the queasiness.

Within minutes the flight attendant returned with the hot brew. Karen stirred in the powdered creamer and took a sip. *This was a mistake. I can't drink it. Should've ordered milk or tea.* She tapped Bobby on the shoulder.

"Honey, I don't want this coffee. I'm sorry I ordered it. Would you like it?"

She stuck the thermal cup in front of his face.

"*You* . . . not want your morning coffee? And I'm really surprised you refused the doughnut or muffin offer. You must be sick." He took the coffee.

"Not sick, just a little nervous."

"About what?"

"Oh, just things on my mind."

"You'll feel fine when you get to the mall and start shopping."

Karen was nervous about keeping a secret from Bobby. She would not have time for much shopping. After Bobby dropped her off at the mall she was going to take a cab to the doctor's office and back. She hoped the timing would work out.

The commercial plane cruised at a much higher altitude than the single-engine Cessna. The beauty of the Canadian wilderness was not as apparent from 30,000 feet. So Karen closed her eyes for the duration of the one-hour flight to Winnipeg. Sleep was not possible—the fishermen were too vociferous about their adventures on the lake that week, their hits and misses with the big ones. But she could mentally rehearse what she would say to Bobby when the time and place were right.

Her vision of sitting across from her husband in a gourmet restaurant with soft music playing was abruptly shattered when an electrical bolt shot through her body. She drew in a quick breath and sat upright.

Meredith! Something has happened to Meredith! Oh, God, help her! Please don't let anything bad happen to her.

She took several deep breaths and tried to calm herself down. The sensation was so strong she had difficulty rationalizing it. Was it a dream? Repressed anxiety about leaving her daughter alone to run the lodge? Or was it just some unreasonable fear arising from her present physical condition? She once read about a team of Russian scientists who hooked a mother rabbit up to some electrodes, took her babies to the other side of the world, and, in a submarine underwater, killed the baby rabbits at a prescribed time. Back in Russia, at the exact moment of their death, electrical impulses from the mother went wild.

If Meredith was in trouble, she knew she couldn't do anything about it now. She would have to keep her appointment in Winnipeg and hope and pray her maternal instincts proved wrong.

* * *

Karen had been sitting in the doctor's office for more than a quarter of an hour. She had leafed through a couple of magazines without absorbing anything her eyes had focused on, except her watch. She kept glancing at the time. She had to be out of there and back at the mall when Bobby came to pick her up.

"Mrs. Marsten?" the nurse's assistant was smiling at her. Karen gave a blood and a urine sample then was escorted to an examination room where she took off her clothes and sat wrapped in a cotton cover-up for another few minutes before Dr. Fuller finally made his appearance. He had her lie down on the table, poked and prodded her, and stuck things in various orifices before leaving the room with a promise to return soon with his findings. Or rather his confirmation of what Karen already knew.

Karen took her clothes off the wall hook and re-dressed. With no book or magazine, she entertained herself by looking around the examination room. A jar of instruments in sterile liquid and a prescription pad sat on the otherwise bare desk. The paper covering of the examination table bore wrinkles where she had lain. Karen eyed the stirrups on each side. *No fun, those humiliating things.* Then she glanced at a calendar on the wall over the desk and her heart began to pound. Above the month of August the featured photograph depicted the upper torso of a wolf howling, his muzzled lifted, eyes closed, mouth open. *Wolfie.* A wave of anxiety fanned out in her chest. *What is the matter with me? I don't remember these scary feelings before, this fear of I-don't-know-what, this premonition of doom.* A knock, and the door opened.

"You are in excellent health, Mrs. Marsten. I can't foresee any problem with this pregnancy. But because of your previous miscarriage, I know you are concerned. Try not to worry. We'll monitor you closely for the next seven months."

"What about my age? I'll be forty my next birthday. I'm afraid I'm too old to bear a child. Will the baby be normal?"

"If this were your first child I would be more concerned. Let me assure you that you are still within child-bearing years. Of course, pregnancy at any age involves a risk. I can't promise any mother that her child will be perfect. But the odds are in favor of a healthy young woman like yourself."

Karen fears were somewhat assuaged by the doctor's words, but she was a worrier. She knew she had inherited that particular trait from her mother. *I'll have to take really good care of myself. Eat more vegetables, no fried food, no coffee—how can I function without morning coffee? I did it once before, I guess I can do it again. Try to be less like Mama and more like Daddy—optimistic but sensible.*

Dr. Fuller calculated that the baby would be born in mid-March. Like Meredith, like the twin boys would have been if she had not lost them that horrible day in October almost ten years ago. She managed to overcome the trauma of it, at least live with it, but Steve did not. Despite all the warning signs and symptoms, her husband's suicide was a complete shock to the whole family. Everyone wanted to know why. Why would such a promising young professor and scholar want to end his life? The note he left—in the arms of Meredith's birthday panda bear—indicated that his unpublished book, the end of his professorship, and the loss of unborn twin sons were the reasons. Karen never understood why he blamed himself for her miscarriage. A bleak period in her life that this unexpected pregnancy was evoking.

"Thank you, Dr. Fuller." Karen tried to force unpleasant memories out of her head and concentrate on the joy the news would bring to Bobby. *After all the years of trying, it would of course happen when we gave up hope and quit even thinking about it.* When she missed her period, she had considered the possibility of terminating the pregnancy without Bobby's knowledge, but her Bible Belt upbringing immediately dismissed the idea as sinful deceit and the taking of a life. Besides, she couldn't, she wouldn't, be unfair to Bobby. Although he was more of a father to Meredith than Steve had ever been, he had no children of his own. He had given her a new beginning in life after Steve's death. And he had loved her devotedly throughout her ten-year marriage to his cousin, without revealing that love to a living soul, keeping it a total secret even from her, especially from her, until in her loneliness and loss she had reached out to him.

The visit to the doctor's office had taken more time than she anticipated. She had done no shopping, and Bobby was probably sitting in the rental car waiting for her at the main entrance to Polo Park Mall, expecting her to appear laden with armloads of boxes and plastic bags. She would have to explain then and there. A rental car in a busy shopping mall parking lot—not exactly the romantic venue she had envisioned for bearing the good tidings of great joy. But she knew that when she told him, circumstances would be irrelevant. Nothing could spoil Bobby's happiness.

* * *

"Can't figure it, Willie. The engine has started cutting out on me. The last couple flights it happened twice. I had to land without power flying into Baldwin yesterday. Came in with the Marstens on Big Bear to see if you could help me out."

Paul stood in front of the aviation mechanic's desk. Willie was the best and, as a result, had a ton of work, but he never seemed busy or rushed. The desk was a jumbled mass of papers, with wrenches, pliers, channel locks, and other assorted tools acting as paper weights. Willie lifted his Connor Aviation Services cap by the frayed bill, ran his hand over his balding hair line and resettled the cap into the ridge it had worn all around his monk-like head.

"I hear Bobby's selling off some outposts. Season must be about over up at Baldwin."

Willie didn't seem too concerned about the engine trouble nor understand the urgency of dealing with it. But Willie was always one to take his time.

"Yeah, the outposts are closed, but I need to get the Cessna back here for the winter."

"Sounds like you got a problem with water in the fuel line, buddy."

"That's what I thought. But I've done everything I know to do. The fuel's not the problem—we still get it from you guys, so . . ."

"So you need me to go up and take a look."

"If there's any way . . . you know Bobby would take care of expenses and do right by you financially."

"Bobby's a good man." Willie lifted his cap again. When he had settled it back into position he swiveled in his seat and looked out the window behind him, pondering something. He swiveled back around.

"I wouldn't do it for anybody else, but, tell you what. I think I can free up this afternoon. Come back about three and we'll take the Connor Beechcraft on up there and I'll see what I can do."

"That'd be terrific. I knew I could count on you for help. I'm going to grab a bite of lunch down the street. Be back well before three." Paul turned toward the door then wheeled back around. "Oh, Willie. I almost forgot. I need a new battery for the ELT. The old one's dead, and I don't have a spare."

* * *

It was probably the most romantic dinner date Karen ever had. A corner table at Romano's Ristorante Italiano with tiny fresh flowers surrounding a lighted tea candle. No champagne or wine, of course, but Bobby held her hands across the table while love and joy poured from his eyes into hers.

"Are you feeling okay?"

"I'm fine, Bobby"

"You're beautiful."

"I'm going to get fat, you know."

"Being pregnant is different from being fat."

"You're right. It sure feels different . . . as well as I remember."

"Will we still be able to make love?"

"Of course, silly! Maybe not during the last month or so, but even then . . ."

The waiter interrupted this highly intellectual conversation and sat a plate of veal marsala in front of Karen, lasagna in front of Bobby. Karen would never eat lasagna again. She had made a big plate of it for dinner the night of Steve's death. She could not see this popular Italian dish without remembering. But Bobby didn't know that detail, and Karen was determined not to let the memory ruin the moment.

There was not a lot of conversation during the meal. Bobby would take a few forkfuls of lasagna then look across the table at her with adoration in his eyes while his lips formed an enigmatic Mona Lisa smile. She returned the smile.

"Don't let me forget to call Meredith when we get back to the hotel." Karen took the last bite of their shared cannoli and wiped her mouth on the bright red napkin. "I've been meaning to ask you something, Honey. Why did Paul come into Winnipeg on Big Bear? Wasn't he supposed to fly the Cessna down when he left camp for the year?"

* * *

Bobby carefully ushered Karen through the revolving door of the Sheraton Hotel.

"Now, watch your step."

Since Karen made the announcement, he had become unduly solicitous of her health and well-being. The rest of the evening she had been subjected to "Let me get that door for you," "Now, be careful, there's a step here," "I'll carry that for you," and the like.

If this keeps up for the next few months I'll go nuts. Once he gets used to the idea and sees that I don't need any special help with my life, maybe he'll settle down.

Inside the lobby he took Karen's arm, guided her toward the elevator, and pressed the button with the up arrow.

He's undoubtedly worried that the elevator door might close on my as-yet-perfectly-flat tummy.

"Mr. Marsten?" They both turned around. The desk clerk, a young Asian with a pleasant round face dressed in a close-fitting dark suit, came up to them. "There's a message for you. I think it's urgent." He handed Bobby an envelope. Bobby opened it and read. He stuffed the envelope and paper into his side pocket just as the elevator door opened. They stepped inside.

"We have to call the lodge immediately."

"It's Meredith. Something's happened to her, I know."

"Please stay calm, Sweetheart."

"I didn't tell you at the time, but on the flight this morning I had an overwhelming premonition that Meredith was in trouble. I wasn't even thinking about her or the lodge, I swear. It just hit me so clearly. I tried but couldn't shake the idea. What does the note say?"

Bobby handed it to her.

Please call the lodge as soon as you get in. Urgent.—Paul

The elevator door slid open. Karen hurried down the hall to their room and waited while Bobby swiped the key card.

She insisted on making the call. Bobby didn't argue. Sitting on the edge of the desk chair, she dialed the lodge's number. Paul answered.

"Paul, it's Karen. What's happened?"

"Meredith evidently took off in the Cessna this morning not long after you left. She hasn't returned."

"Does anybody know where she went?"

"Emil said she came through the kitchen early this morning, made herself some sandwiches, and went out the back. Shortly after that he heard the plane take off. Assumed it was me. She wasn't anywhere around when Willie and I got here and found the Cessna missing. When there was still no sign of her at supper, we started trying to reach you."

"Did she file a flight plan?"

"We're checking on that. In any case, you need to be at Connor Air tomorrow morning at five. They'll have a pilot ready to fly you up."

Karen put the phone back in place but kept one hand on the receiver. She cradled her forehead in the other as she repeated what Paul had said.

"You were right, Bobby. We never should have left her with the responsibility of the lodge. It's my fault for wanting to come with you. I should have stayed there with her."

Bobby came over and knelt on one knee beside his wife. He took her hand off the phone and pressed it between his palms.

"It's not your fault. I know it's hard, but try not to let yourself get upset. I'll find her, Sweetheart, I promise you. I think I know where she went."

"But do you know why she hasn't come home?"

Sleep was impossible. Karen paced the hotel room, clock-watching. At three a.m. low rumblings and sharp flashes of light signaled an approaching storm. She pulled the desk chair to the window, tugged on the plastic rods to part the heavy curtain a bit, and sat staring at the droplets hitting hard against the plate glass. Ominous clouds so deep a gray that they appeared blue rolled in like malevolent spirits intent on spreading doom.

"Raining?" Bobby threw back the covers and perched on the edge of the bed.

"Storming. Just started."

He joined her at the window to see for himself. Karen scrutinized his facial expression in an effort to decipher his assessment of flying conditions.

"How bad is it? Can we fly in this?"

Bobby tightened his lips and drew in an audible breath through them. "Ceiling's really low. Hard to say. By five it could lift. Let's just get over there. I can tell better when we are outside." He reached for his jeans and pulled them on over his boxers. Karen had not undressed from last night. Her one carry-on bag was packed and ready to go, toothbrush and all. Bobby headed for the bathroom. Karen heard the shower running.

Downstairs in the lobby the desk clerk, the same Asian fellow, promptly called for a taxi. Karen's breath was fast and shallow, her heart pounding in her ears. She and Bobby took a seat on an overstuffed sofa and waited in grim silence for what seemed an eternity until the Duffy Cab arrived. The ride to Connor through heavy rain was even longer. Karen wondered if Bobby's silence indicated that there was no chance of flying out. As if he knew what she was thinking, he reached over and took her hand in an attempt at reassurance, but Karen sensed his anxiety.

The pilot met them at the door. A heavy guy with a bowling ball of a gut hanging over his low-slung belt. A two-day growth of beard.

"I'm Pete Sanders. Come on in. I've got a pot of coffee brewing. We may have a little delay, but we'll take off as soon as this front passes through."

In spite of his efforts at good will, the man did not inspire Karen's confidence.

"What's the forecast?" Bobby cut to the chase.

"Latest I heard, it'll ease up by noon."

Dispensing with civilities, Bobby brushed past the pilot and marched straight into the office where static from the broadband radio hissed between vocal pronouncements.

"He's a pilot, too, and has to hear it for himself." Karen's southern genteel manners kicked in, despite her initial reaction to the man.

When Bobby emerged from the office, Karen detected a bit of relief on his face.

"I spoke with Paul again. He called Civil Air Search and Rescue, and they sent a rescue plane out. Willie's out there, too."

"Well, looks like they've got it under control, Ma'am. Willie will find her for you. You want some coffee now? I think it's ready. May not be too good, though. I'm not much of a cook."

Karen had no desire to talk. She didn't want coffee. Angry at the weather and impotent to do anything about it, she paced, stopping to peer out every time she passed a window. After she had logged in about fifty miles around the room, Bobby came over, put his arm around her shoulders and whispered.

"Sweetheart, let's get something to eat. You'll need your strength. I know you're worried, so am I. But there's nothing more that can be done right now."

"Worried? Bobby, I'm scared to death. Do you think I can eat?"

"Maybe you're not hungry, but you have another child to think of."

Chapter Six

Meredith put the matches back into her pocket. The fire could wait. *After all, this is what I came for.* She stood up and began to call.

"Wol--------fie! Oh, Wol-------fie! Here, boy! Wol----------fie!"

She waited, then called again and again, walking up and down the sandy crescent of the little beach. She stopped to examine an opening in the bushes that seemed to her to be the beginning of an animal path.

"Not big enough for a bear. Probably made by a small creature like a fox or marten or raccoon coming to drink water." She bit her lower lip and thought for a minute. "I bet Wolfie uses it. Maybe it will take me to him." Driven by this idea, she ducked into the foliage to follow wherever the path led.

"Wol------fie! Come on, boy! Here, Wolfie!"

She crouched her way along what she assumed was the animal path, distancing herself farther and farther from the lake. She was relieved when, after a while, the path became more like a human trail and she could walk upright. But the footing was tough. Each step took some thought and effort. There were places where the trail was blocked by a bush or a fallen tree trunk. She pushed her way around, over, or under every obstacle. At one point she wasn't sure whether the trail went to the left, right, or straight ahead. She thought she heard a swishing sound, a sound of quiet movement. She stopped. The sound stopped. She continued walking. The sound picked up again. Something—or someone—was following her. She called Wolfie, thinking maybe it was him and he didn't fully recognize her.

The noise eventually stopped, as did the trail. Meredith encountered an impasse of fallen trees and thick brambles. The path simply ended. *I must have gone off the trail somewhere. I'll backtrack.* But nothing around her seemed familiar. *How did I get here?* She tried one way then another, and yet another, getting her sense of direction more and more confused until she was completely disoriented. Not being able to see the sky through the canopy of thick spruces and pines made keeping her bearings more difficult. She had no idea how to return to the beach and her waiting stack of firewood. She had no idea who or what had followed her. What she did know was that she was unlikely to be rescued anytime soon, or even at all, and that she had intruded into some bear's territory, a bear with jaws powerful enough to chew through a metal float.

"I should have marked the trail as I went—like Bobby taught me to do. Why can't I think clearly?" she asked the silence around her. Her breathing became short and fast. She felt fear and anxiety engulfing her with the wilderness. As if she had entered Danté's underworld, she abandoned all hope, sat down at the base of a white spruce, put her head in her hands, and gave way to the emotions of the Little Girl Lost. Tears ran between her fingers and down her arms, sobs heaved in her chest and throat.

* * *

"Are you okay? Can I help?"

With an audible gasp Meredith leapt to her feet and found herself facing a human being. Her heart pounding in her ears, her breath fast and shallow, she stared at the figure in front of her. A young man about nineteen or twenty years old with tan skin as smooth as pebblestones and long black hair that shone like moonlight on dark water. Eyes of an eagle, deep and sharp. He wore jeans, a deerskin jacket, and high-top moccasins tied around the bottom of his pants. A large beaded bag hung across his chest.

"I didn't mean to frighten you. I've been following you for a while, mainly out of curiosity, but also thought you might be lost."

"I--I am, sort of." Meredith bent her head and discretely wiped her wet cheeks.

"How did you get here?"

"I flew in yesterday."

"Where's your pilot?"

"I'm the pilot. I flew myself in."

"You're a pilot? I'm impressed. By the way, I'm Mark." He extended his arm in greeting.

"Meredith." She offered him a shaky tear-drenched hand.

"You must be the Marsten girl from Baldwin Lake."

"That's right." *Who is this person and what is he doing here?* She felt relieved but still uneasy that this man had followed her.

"My grandfather works part time for Mr. Marsten—his name is Tom. You probably know him."

"Of course. So you're Tom's grandson. You're Ojibwe."

"I am."

Meredith's heart slowed and her breathing deepened. "He has told us a little about you. He's seems very fond of you."

"As I am of him. He and my grandmother taught me practically everything I know about the wilderness and about our people, the culture, and the language."

Meredith regretted that Mark had caught her at her lowest moment, but was glad that being a pilot had somewhat rescued her dignity.

"And who is Wolfie? . . . if you don't mind my asking."

"My wolf."

"Your what?"

"Well, he *was* my wolf until a couple of months ago. We released him back into the wild."

"How did you get this wolf? Was he caught in a trap?"

She told Mark a brief synopsis of the saga of Wolfie, from the starving pup to his return to the wild.

"I flew up to check on him, if I can find him. But he didn't come when I called, so either he's no longer here or he has already forgotten about me."

"So I guess you'll fly back to the lodge."

"Well, . . . I can't."

That remark necessitated another explanation. She told him about the storm, the loss of power and the radio, and the forced landing, even about the bear chewing holes in the float during the night. She omitted the part about flying off alone without her parents' permission or knowledge.

"You've been through quite an ordeal. You must be pretty tired . . . and hungry. Do you have any food with you?"

"I had some, but I ate most of it and somehow lost the rest. And yes, I am tired and hungry. But you haven't told me what *you're* doing here in the middle of nowhere." Meredith felt it was his turn to do some explaining.

Mark put one foot on a log and rested his forearm on his upper leg.

"Well, you see, my grandfather—and my grandmother—spent their summers living in the bush like our ancestors. As I grew up they taught me how to survive in the wilderness. Not only learning to survive, but mainly to experience the joy of being a part of it, of living in harmony with nature and with our ancient traditions. That's why I'm here. This is my third summer alone in the bush. I guess that sounds foolish to you."

"Not at all, Mark. I'm not an aboriginal, but I've spent eight summers at the lodge. I've learned a lot about the wilderness from my step-father. I can't remember a time in my life when I wasn't part of it. So I know exactly what you mean."

Mark's lips parted in a smile that showed in his eyes as well. He straightened up. "It's getting late, you know. The nocturnal critters will be out and about soon. Come with me to my camp. I have plenty of food—and shelter for the night. And tomorrow I'll go with you to find Wolfie, if you like."

"I don't want to disrupt your solitude."

"You're not disrupting anything at all. It gets pretty lonely out here. I'm happy to have some company—especially a girl who's also a pilot and a rescuer of wolves."

Mark's honest face, his disarming smile, and his friendly manner lay to rest the vestiges of her apprehension.

"You have to go past this big old chokecherry bush to stay on the trail." He pushed around it and held it back, waiting for her to join him.

She zipped up her jacket against the increasing night chill, pulled the straps of her backpack over her shoulders, and followed the Ojibwe deeper into the woods.

* * *

She found the footing difficult. They were obviously following some sort of trail, but the ground was not solid. With each step her hiking boots sank an inch or two into eons of natural debris from the trees and shrubs and made an audible cracking sound. It was the first time she had paid attention to the sound of her own footsteps. She stopped walking.

I wouldn't be able to hear any animal approaching—human or otherwise.

She listened. Mark kept going a few more paces then stopped, realizing his female guest was no longer following. He turned around.

"Something wrong?"

"No. I was just listening"

"To what?"

"To the silence . . . I mean to the lack of sound of your footsteps. I make enough noise to alert every bear within miles. How do you do that, or rather keep from doing that? Is it your moccasins?"

Mark looked at her feet then at his.

"Yes, partly. It has more to do with the way you put your weight on your feet when you walk. Most people dig their heel in first then roll forward onto the ball of the foot then the toe. Like this."

In a slightly exaggerated manner he demonstrated the "normal" way to take a step. It made a clear crunching sound. Meredith took a few steps in a circle just to verify.

*He's right. That **is** the way I walk.*

"Well, now show me your way."

"Watch. You distribute your weight evenly over the entire foot. Don't let your leg press the foot down too fast into the forest floor."

Mark took a few silent steps toward her. Immediately she tried to imitate him. She crunched less, but her steps were still audible.

Mark laughed at her fledging efforts. "It's not easy to do. It'll take some practice. I learned it from childhood. It's second nature to me now."

"I imagine being able to walk silently in the woods is pretty important to survival."

"It surely is. We still have a little way to go before we reach my camp. You can practice."

"You don't happen to have a spare pair of moccasins on you? Ladies, size 6."

They resumed the trek and, as she tried to walk with silent steps, a little bubble of joy began to form in Meredith's heart.

* * *

It was dusk when they reached Mark's camp. Luminosity from low in the western sky had managed to penetrate into the forest, casting indigo hues over the area Mark had made his wilderness home. Meredith took a few steps into the clearing and made a slow 380-degree turn.

"Wow. Did you do this by yourself?"

"Tom helped me at first. He picked the spot. It's protected from the wind, not far from the lake, and has a natural stream—in other words, running water."

"And you cook on an open fire over there?" She pointed to a ring of stones surrounding a blackened area. A heavy pot hung suspended from a primitive wooden rack.

"That's an awesome pot. Doesn't the rack catch on fire?"

"It has been known to," Mark admitted.

"I'd be afraid the iron pot would, like, collapse into the fire if it were full of stew or soup or something."

"That's been known to happen, too."

Meredith couldn't repress her laughter at his true confessions. *This guy is pretty cool. He's funny. And good-looking. He has succeeded in putting me at ease in the middle of a horrendous situation. He just may have saved my life.*

"Let me show you around. Oh, and please feel free to ask questions or make any critical comments."

Meredith loved his irony. "I will."

We've spent probably no more than an hour together and we're already setting the tone of our relationship. Relationship? With someone I just met in the middle of the wilderness? But I do know his family. Sort of.

Once again she found herself following Mark like a puppy as he explained the set up of his camp.

I wonder what the sleeping arrangements will be tonight. I hope he doesn't think that by coming here with him I would . . . .

* * *

Mark's camp, set in a small clearing alongside a stream, consisted of a wigwam-like structure made of birch bark, a large fire pit, a skinning rack formed out of five denuded poplar branches—two planted at angles in the ground at each end and lashed together with bark strips at the top to form forks, and one horizontal pole lying in the forks. An ax lodged in the cut cylinder of a large tree trunk stood next to piles of split wood. Several bags made of animal skins along with two or three plastic ones dangled on ropes strung over a tree limb.

"What's in the bags?" Meredith asked.

"That's my pantry. Best way to keep food away from animals."

"Like bears?"

"Among others." Mark smiled.

"Plastic is not exactly ancestral."

"I make some concessions to modern life. Want something to eat?"

"I wouldn't mind. Actually, to tell the truth I'm famished."

"Actually, to tell the truth, I am, too." Mark went to the tree trunk where one of the ropes was fastened to a bottom branch, unwound it, and lowered the bag. "We have smoked beaver and Oreo cookies."

"The best of both worlds!"

Meredith's comment provoked spontaneous laughter from both of them, an honest, good-natured chuckle that eradicated any misgivings she entertained about this young man. Mark pulled a folding camp chair out of the wigwam for Meredith and handed her a tin plate full of both worlds. He sat cross-legged on the grass beside her.

"Tell me about yourself. Do you go to school?" Meredith asked then bit into a tender piece of beaver meat.

"I'll be a senior at the University of Winnipeg in just a few weeks. I'm in the Aboriginal Culture Program. I'm hoping to replace my grandfather when he retires from teaching at the Indian Culture Center in Winnipeg. My parents both worked long hours at several jobs to make ends meet. My mother died when I was still a kid, so my grandparents really raised me. They instilled in me the respect for our people's ancient ways, our traditions, our bond with the wilderness. Both of them—nakomis and mashomis —used to spend most of the summer in the bush, over on Poplar River. When I made the decision to do the same, I chose this area near the lake we call *wagosh zaaga'igan*—Fox Lake, the lake where you landed. What do you call it?"

"I don't know of any name, or even a number. What made you pick this particular place?"

"I spent the first summer with Tom at his camp. It's not far from Bobby's outpost on Poplar River. But I wanted something really remote, away from everything—no logging roads, outposts, lodges, or fly-in fishing lakes. I don't think too many people even know about this lake—just a few aboriginals and, unfortunately some poachers."

"Ever run into any—poachers, I mean?"

"No, but I've seen their handiwork."

Rather than continue his story, Mark took a few more bites of food, chewed it intently, staring at her all the while.

"I like your hair, you know." he said.

"My hair?"

"Yes. The tawny curls sticking out from under your cap."

Meredith removed the cap and shook her head to loosen the curls and show off her thick brown mane. "And I like your long, straight black hair." Meredith threw her head back, lowering her eyelids and parting her lips in a coquettish smile. *Am I flirting with this guy? Here in the middle of nowhere? Under these dire circumstances? I know I'm in big trouble with Mama and Bobby, and probably with the authorities, too. Oh well, make the best of a bad situation, as Mama always says.*

Mark got to his feet. He took their plates and walked down a path that led to a stream, Meredith followed and watched him rinse them then bring them back to the wigwam.

"It's turning a little cool. I usually get a campfire going in the evenings—that's traditional." Meredith got the implication.

Within minutes the firewood was flaming and popping in the pit before them, dispelling the chill of nightfall. He removed the ax from the chopping block and dragged the large cylinder of wood over to the fire beside Meredith, and sat on it.

"Your turn to tell me about yourself."

She began her story the way he had begun his. "I'm entering my senior year in high school, I'm a huge hockey fan, I hate TV and electronic games—that makes my classmates think I'm weird. I *do* have a cell phone—it doesn't work up here, of course. I *do* use the computer, mostly to email friends, not for Facebook and junk like that. I really love to fly the seaplane and I really love to fish—I think I'm pretty good at both."

"Where do you plan to attend college?"

"My mother wants me to go to Heyward College in South Carolina—where my father was a professor. I could live with my grandparents there in Spring Hill—that's where the college is. Bobby—my stepfather—went to the University of Iowa, so I want to check that out, too."

"You probably haven't yet started thinking about a major."

"I have, actually. I want to go into Wildlife Management, like my stepfather, maybe work in some national park in the U.S. or a provincial park in Canada, anywhere I can find a job like, you know, putting bands and collars on wild animals and tracking them, you know, to learn more about them and help preserve them."

"Do you have a boyfriend?"

Mark's abrupt question sent the blood rushing to her cheeks. *If I say yes, he'll lose interest. If I say no, he'll think I must be weird for real and totally undesirable.*

"I haven't had much time for boyfriends. For the past two years I've been involved with raising my wolf. He's my buddy, my best friend."

Once on the subject of Wolfie, Meredith launched into a more detailed account of the entire Wolfie episode in her life, from the moment she took the pup into her arms all the way to the parting embrace. For some reason she wanted Mark to understand how much the wolf meant to her.

Mark reached out for her hand and cradled it in both of his. "There is an old saying about wolves: you may feed the wolf as much as you like, but he will always glance toward the forest. You did the right thing."

He released her hands and patted her on the knee. "We'll go looking for him tomorrow. You can sleep on my pallet tonight. I'll put a blanket down out here. I do that on warm nights. The restroom is any convenient spot in the woods. I'll stand guard—with my back turned." Meredith marveled at his ease of handling touchy situations.

Once nestled in his primitive bearskin bed, she breathed deeply and slowly to absorb the purity of nature that surrounded her. Her heart beat in tempo with an ancient rhythm emanating from somewhere in the core of the earth, an intense pulsation of life found only in pristine nature, unchanged since the beginning of time. It felt right for her to be here where life and death abounded in equal temperament. It felt as it should be, as it really was. Not the Garden of Eden, no terrestrial paradise where the lamb could lie down with the lion or a child play near the adder's den, but a purposed, planned balance of all things animal, vegetable, and mineral, where her part in its cyclical pattern was no more nor less than that of the wild dandelion or the fully-racked bull moose.

* * *

She awoke to the chirping of boreal chicadees and the crackling of the rekindled fire. She had slept well. She tried to remember her strange and startling dream about Mark and Wolfie, but she couldn't. Only the feeling of belonging, of being loved, and then being forcefully separated. That was all of the dream that remained with her. She sat up just as Mark ducked into the wigwam with a steaming cup in his hand.

"Have some raspberry tea. It'll wake you up."

"Thanks, Mark." She accepted the brew and sipped on the hot liquid. "I bet it's traditional."

"You're right." Mark nodded and winked.

My God, he winked at me. Is he flirting, too? Or am I imagining things?

Meredith had slept fully clothed, so all she had to do was put on her hiking boots and lace them up, make a quick solo trip to the wilderness restroom, run her fingers through her curls, and she was ready to start the day.

"What's for breakfast?"

"No more blueberries, no more blackberries this time of year. We'll have to make do with wild rice."

"That's fine with me."

Mark dished out the rice from an aluminum pot steaming away on the campfire grate.

"Ummm. It's sweet."

"I put a little maple syrup in it. Like it?"

"I love it." Meredith blew on her spoon to cool the next mouthful. I love the plastic bowls, too. They remind me of civilization."

"Yea. I like the silver spoons, myself." Mark grinned as he put a spoonful of rice in his mouth. "Better eat up. We have a long trek today." He ladled another scoop into her bowl.

After breakfast, Meredith volunteered to clean the dishes. Although she expected the water to be shallow this late in the summer, she was surprised by the force of the flow. It gurgled around fallen branches and hissed over rock beds. She found a spot where a strong current ran between two boulders. She sat on one of them and, with a firm grip, held out the bowls and silverware one by one for Mother Nature to wash.

I think I could live out here for a while—not by myself, but if I had somebody like Mark with me . . . . Though Mark couldn't see her, much less hear what she was thinking, Meredith felt herself blushing.

When she returned from the stream, Mark handed her a stick of something that resembled a miniature corn cob.

"Here. Chew on this. It'll brush your teeth."

"Okay. Sure." Meredith took the stick and began to gnaw, hoping that her nonchalance made her appear accustomed to life in the bush. She hadn't a clue as to what it was. "Now can we go find Wolfie?" she asked, still gnawing.

Mark packed his beaded bag with foodstuffs then strapped a knife around his waist. "I'm ready if you are."

"Don't you have a gun?"

"I have one I use for hunting."

"Shouldn't we bring it along . . . just in case . . . we meet up with a *you-know-what*? Like a mother and cubs."

"Okay, if you're willing to carry it sometimes." Mark ducked into the wigwam and returned holding a rifle by the barrel. "Are you sure?"

"I'm sure."

He extended it to her. "Here you go, Wild Bill. You can be the first to carry it. Just don't shoot me."

"You mean it's loaded?"

"Never know when you might need it in a hurry."

"Well, thanks for the reassuring advice."

Pulling on her backpack and slipping the rifle strap over one shoulder, Meredith set out with her new-found friend on a quest for a certain wolf somewhere out there in the Canadian wilderness.

Chapter Seven

It wasn't until 3:15 p.m. that the twin-engine Beechcraft finally touched down on the hard-surface runway of Bolton Lake Lodge. Karen had dared to hope that Meredith would be there to greet her when she and Bobby alighted. She found only Paul and the cook waiting on the airstrip. The four of them watched as the Connor Air Services pilot revved the engines, taxied down to the far end of the runway, did a one-hundred-eighty degree turn, and came roaring past them, dust billowing out behind. Once he had lifted off and headed out over the lake, the noise level subsided. Paul turned to Bobby.

"They're still out there looking, the rescue plane with two men and Willie, but no sign of . . . ."

"Haven't they picked up the signal from the ELT?" Bobby cut him off.

Paul grimaced and lowered his head. "That's just it. The transmitter battery was low. I picked up two new ones in Winnipeg at Connor. That was one of the reasons I went, and to see if I could get Willie to take a look at the engine. It's cut out on me a couple of times recently . . ."

"And you left a plane with an engine problem and probably no ELT? Obviously Meredith didn't know anything about it." Bobby let out an audible breath and swept his fingers through his hair.

"Can we reach the rescue pilots on the broadband?" Karen looked desperately at Paul.

"Should be able to."

"Bobby, talk to them. Tell them where she is. You said you knew," Karen pleaded. *She was gone all night. Frightened and alone.*

"That's exactly what I intend to do right now. I'll give them the coordinates of the lake where we left the wolf. She's bound to be there." He hurried up the path toward the main building and into the office, Karen on his heels.

But Bobby couldn't give them the coordinates. The map was gone.

* * *

Afternoon turned into evening. Karen felt helpless. She wanted to be out looking for her daughter—her only child. *I can't believe this is happening. It's all my fault. I should have paid attention to Bobby's concern about leaving her in charge. I should have made them turn the Big Bear around and bring me back. I knew something bad was going to happen to her.*

She was a "fixer." Whatever was wrong, she always believed she could fix it, and she almost always did. One summer she and Steve found the cabin at Poplar River outpost overrun with mice. She had torn apart the cardboard food cartons and built a corridor through which the mice were successfully corralled out the front door. She was used to fixing wrong notes and wrong rhythms in her piano students' playing. She sewed up Meredith's beloved Pooh Bear when a seam opened and stuffing came out. For years now she had dealt with guests' various concerns at the lodge—and she always found solutions to any problem they had. But there was nothing she could do to "fix" this.

She paced around the large dining area, looking out at the lake every few seconds, hoping to see a rescue plane heading in—with Meredith aboard. As minutes turned into hours, Karen gave up trying to think of something *she* could do to find her daughter. In a whisper she called on a higher power.

"Please, Lord, forgive me for allowing this terrible thing to happen. Please don't let my neglect cause Meredith to suffer harm. I promise I will be more attentive to her from now on. And I will listen to my God-given intuition and act on it. Just please, please, bring her back safely to me. She's a sweet, innocent child. And I know you love the little children."

Though not a Catholic by faith, Karen made the sign of the cross, hoping that it would add some weight to her prayer. She wiped her wet cheeks with the back of her hand and went to the sliding glass doors to look out again. A plane was coming in.

* * *

Bobby rechecked all cabinets and drawers in the office but couldn't locate the map anywhere. He sat at the desk for a minute, his mind going in ten different directions at once, while the battery-operated wall clock clicked away the seconds. He *had* to do something. He couldn't just sit here by the radio waiting and hoping, trying to decipher the static exchanges between Willie and the rescue plane. Desperate for fresh air, he left the office and went back down to the floatplane dock. He filled his lungs with the cool air and looked out over the lake. *Willie is out there, a rescue plane is out there, but I'm stuck here with no plane.* The surface of the water was muddled by a low wind out of the east. Clouds in mixed shades of gray accompanied the wind. Something about watching the cloud formations in the vast expanse above the lake made Bobby think of the one thing he could do. He spoke aloud, without taking his eyes off the sky.

"Lord God, you know I'm not really the praying type. I figure you are too busy with the bigger problems of the world to be bothered by my little needs and wants. I try to take care of those things by myself. So far I've done okay. But this time I really need your help. I know it's my fault that Meredith is by herself in the wilderness. I know the dangers she faces. But I'm the one who taught her to fly. I made her return the wolf she loved. And I left her here to take on responsibility that I knew was too much for her. Lord, I ask you in your mercy to forgive me for doing so. Please keep her safe and help us find her. You have given me so much—the only woman I could ever love, the wilderness life I love, a great lodge to run, the very, very special step-daughter of the man I loved as a brother, and now you have chosen to bless me with my own child soon. Please hear my prayer. Bring her back to us. I promise I will be a caring and watchful father to her. I love her and her mother so much . . . ."

The lump that had grown in his throat as he prayed made it impossible for him to continue. The act of speaking to the Creator made him begin to take stock of his own beliefs. He went to church whenever and wherever Karen was asked to substitute for a regular organist or pianist. But his church was not a building, his religion was not manifested in hymns, or sermons, or rites of any kind, although he respected them all. His "church" was here, this pristine wilderness, untouched, the way it was created, whether through evolution, a big bang, or God's magical wand. How it came to be was unimportant to him. He could recognize the face of God in every creature he encountered in this church, from the smallest butterfly to the largest black bear. He understood the perfect balance of nature—that creatures preyed upon each other was part of it, that plants were devoured, that trees were felled for beaver lodges and dams—it was as it should be. And he wanted to be part of it. He wanted to preserve it from human abuse, to admire the shape of every leaf and the scamper of every red squirrel, to marvel at all the wonders that he never ceased to find in it. Only a supreme being, an omnipotent, omniscient power could have designed it and brought it into being. Every time he flew over the wilderness, every time he landed or took off on one of its lakes Bobby was in his church. Perhaps Baldwin Lake Lodge was the altar where he worshipped the Creator of all this beauty and perfection.

His meditation was interrupted by the sound of an engine. He scanned the sky in the direction of the sound. A plane was descending through the clouds. Squinting against the luminescence, he recognized the aircraft. The search plane was coming in.

* * *

Karen hurried down to the dock, hope rising hard in her chest as sharp as a knife gouging her lungs. She arrived completely out of breath.

"Are you okay?" Bobby must have sensed her anxiety.

"I'll be fine," she panted.

"It's the rescue plane."

"Oh, dear God, maybe they have her."

"Don't get your hopes up. There was no message to that effect on the radio when I left the office. I'm sure they would have let us know. We'll just see what they have to say."

Bobby's last words were barely audible above the churning of the twin propellers and the sloshing of the water. There were two men aboard, the pilot and another rescue worker. The pilot stayed in his seat while the other man hopped down onto the dock. He was short but muscular and ruddy, like a man used to being outdoors. Both he and the pilot wore the dark blue, short-sleeved uniform of Manitoba's Search-and-Rescue Corps.

"You must be the mother and father. . ."

"Yes, we are." Karen responded before the man had finished.

Bobby grabbed one of the mooring ropes hanging from a wing and held the plane steady while the wake thumped it against the rubber tires lining the sides of the dock.

"What's the situation?" he asked.

"Willie said you might know where she went."

"I'll show you on your map."

"Well, we're ready to head back to Winnipeg, but first thing tomorrow we're sending up a guy named Brad. He's the best in the service. He's got instincts about things, plus he's a great tracker. If you can get him in the general vicinity, he'll find her. Just be here on the dock around five in the morning. He'll have detailed maps. Show him where you think she is." The rescuer turned to Karen. "If anybody can, Brad'll find her, Ma'am. I promise you."

Karen nodded, unable to form a rational response, remembering the same words spoken to her while she and Bobby waited to fly out from Connor in Winnipeg. She remained silent as the man climbed back into the plane. She and her husband stood motionless, watching the seaplane taxi out and take off. The next thing she knew, she was in Bobby's arms, needing to hear his breathing, to feel his heart beating against hers, to smell his familiar woodsy scent, to absorb his strength.

"Oh, Bobby, I feel so helpless. What are we going to do?"

"We're going to eat, get some rest, and be on the dock tomorrow morning at five. And we're flying out with them. We're going to bring Meredith home."

"There is one thing we can do, Honey. And it may help. In fact I think it's the most important thing we can do."

"What do you mean?"

"Well . . . I know you're not much of a church-going person, but I know you believe in God. We can pray . . . I mean, I already have . . ."

"So have I." Bobby squinted and looked away at the horizon. "Maybe I don't go around making a show of my beliefs or even talking about them. That probably makes me look like an atheist or something to most people." He looked back at her. "But don't you know me better than that?"

Karen met his eyes. "You're the best person I've ever known. You demonstrate all the Christian values of the Bible—those listed by Saint Paul in first Corinthians, chapter thirteen, you know, the passage that begins 'Though I speak with the tongues of men and angels and have not charity . . . .' Bobby, you show love all the time, to everyone, even to people who have done you wrong, to people you don't even know. You're a good person, Bobby."

Bobby pulled away and turned squarely towards the water and the dying sun. "How can I be good when I'm living with my brother's wife, a woman I longed for the whole time you two were married? A man whose parents raised me like their own after mine died in that accident?"

"Steve wasn't really your brother. Besides, you never stepped the least bit out of line. And, what's more, it's biblical for a man to marry his brother's wife if the brother dies without a male heir. And he's supposed to give her children, too. And now you have performed that duty, too. Don't you see that it's all been a part of God's plan?"

Bobby turned around, took her hands and pulled her close to him again. "Karen, my sweet love, I think you should have been a preacher rather than a pianist. You're very persuasive."

Karen closed her eyes and just for a moment forgot her lost child, as her husband placed the tenderest of kisses on her lips.

* * *

The sun had dropped below the horizon setting the sky ablaze with scarlet and purple when Willie's amphibious plane landed on Baldwin Lake and taxied to the floatplane dock.

"I checked all the outpost cabins. No sign she's been at any of them," Willie told Bobby and Karen as soon as he climbed down out of the plane. "Civil Air SAR has called off the search for now, but they're sending in a plane first thing tomorrow. They need to have a better idea of what area to search."

"They stopped by here on the way back and told us. As soon as they get here I'll show them exactly where I think she is." Bobby said.

He and Willie continued talking while mooring the plane. But their words grew faint and distorted in Karen's brain. She couldn't bear the thought of another night of fear and anxiety. Another night with her daughter lost in the wilderness or drowning in a lake. Her throat tightened and she gulped back the urge to sob. She felt an arm around her shoulders. Bobby must have sensed her anguish.

"Like I told you, we'll both go with them in the morning. They'll have detailed maps. We'll find her. She's a smart girl and knows how to survive in the wilderness."

Karen could only give her head an affirmative nod. *She is smart, but she did a stupid thing.*

"I remember when her mother insisted on staying alone in the cabin at Poplar River, in spite of my objections."

Yes, but everyone knew where I was. And I was not just sixteen years old. She kept the thoughts to herself.

Bobby turned around to his buddy. "Come on up to the lodge, Willie. You probably need some food and drink. We'll fix you up with some dinner and a comfortable place to stay."

"I slept in the guides' bunk house last night. It's just fine. But I won't say no to a good meal."

He and Willie took the path to the main lodge building. Karen lingered.

"You guys go ahead. I'll be there in a minute."

Bobby gave her a pointed look. "You're sure?"

"Yes." She forced a smile.

The brilliant purples, reds, and golds of the late-summer sunset were reflected in the lake. The air had grown still. A flock of Canada geese flapped passed, black against the flaming sky. But Karen couldn't stay focused on the beauty of nature's spectacle. She shuddered, envisioning her daughter shivering from fright and the chill of approaching night, somewhere out there. For the past twenty-four hours her mind kept constructing images of a Cessna nose-diving into some unknown body of water, a girl strapped in the pilot's seat, unable to free herself before frigid water engulfed her. In another scenario a bear attacked a defenseless child, sinking his teeth into a slender shoulder and raking long claws over a beautiful young face.

She remembered how once she and her first husband, Steve, had become totally lost in the bush, even when they had been so careful to follow a marked trail. And Tom had come to their rescue. *Oh God, please send someone to help her the way you did for us.*

With that hopeful prayer in her heart, she left the dock and hurried to join Willie and her husband.

* * *

Emil had prepared a prime rib dinner, but Karen couldn't eat a bite of the rare meat. She glanced at Bobby's plate. He wasn't exactly scarfing it up either. She nibbled at some gratinéed potatoes, mostly pushing them around with a fork and listening to the conversation between the two men.

"I really appreciate your checking the outposts. That was a smart thing to do. She always loves to go with me whenever I fly out to one. But I know you've got to get back to your job at Connor. You're their ace mechanic." Bobby reached over and gave Willie's shoulder a typical guy's quick "thank you" gesture.

"No way." Willie shook his head and chewed. He had the jowls of a bulldog that pouched out when he filled his mouth. He watched his plate, eager for the next bite, preparing each one, the whole time he spoke. "I'm not going back 'till we locate her and get her home. You know, I've got a teenage daughter myself. You'd do the same for me if the situation were reversed." Willie sawed off a bite of the rib roast and propped the forkful in midair with his elbow. "One time she left to go shopping at Polo Park with some friends, and when she didn't come home for dinner, Peggy—that's my wife—and I got frantic. Both of us jumped in the car." He illustrated by waving the meat in a circle. "We looked all over that mall, asking in every shop if anyone had seen her. Found her in the food court just hanging out, drinking a soda with some other kids. They had met up with a couple of older boys that seemed to be trying to impress these girls—and doing a pretty good job of it. Made 'em forget all about the time." The chunk of beef finally went into the mouth, eyes still on his plate.

Karen sighed. *As if a girl late for dinner and drinking Co-colas in the mall is anything at all compared to Meredith and a float plane disappearing in the wilderness for more than twenty-four hours. Oh, God, forgive me! Willie is trying so hard, I realize that. I just feel so helpless.* With new resolve to demonstrate her gratitude she stood and gathered the three plates, one full, one half full, and one empty.

"Anyone care for dessert? Emil is a great baker. I'm sure he has something real good for us."

"Not me, Mrs. Marsten. I'm a meat and potatoes man. I had plenty, thanks." Willie drained his bottle of beer, wiped his mouth on one of the lodge's dark green cloth napkins, and set it on the table. "In fact, if you'll excuse me, I think I'll turn in. You work hard, you sleep hard, right?" he said to Karen as he pushed away from the table, stood, and turned to Bobby. "I imagine the SAR plane will get in pretty early."

"I think it would be good for all of us to get some sleep," Bobby said. "You won't be alone in the bunk house. Cedrick and Tom just got in about an hour ago from an overnight bear hunt and will probably sleep like logs, too."

After Bobby left to escort Willie to the bunk house, Karen finished clearing the table and took the dishes into the kitchen.

"Thank you for this late dinner, Emil."

"It's okay, Madame. I 'ope you find her tomorrow."

"We will. You know how determined Bobby is when he sets his mind to something." She rinsed the plates and started to put them in the dishwasher.

"No, Madame. Let me take care of the kitchen."

"Emil, if you don't mind, tell me exactly what she did when she came in here."

Listening to Emil's account, Karen visualized her daughter, picking up the biscuits and bacon, going to the bread box then to the refrigerator. She could see the curly head bent over the counter, intent on making turkey sandwiches. She could even smell the mayonnaise, taste the turkey. *She planned it so carefully!* Her breath became short and fast. The room began to swirl around. Karen grabbed the edge of the counter as the meager contents of her stomach spilled onto the kitchen floor.

* * *

"No, Honey. It wasn't so much because of the pregnancy. I just . . . I don't know . . . I think it's just worry. I was talking to Emil and trying to reconstruct what our daughter did in the kitchen yesterday morning. All of a sudden I got dizzy and nauseated."

Bobby sat on the side of the bed next to her. He had checked her forehead for fever, taken her wrist and felt her pulse, and was gently stroking her arm. For the first time in their eight years of marriage Bobby's eyes showed signs of fatigue. That, too, worried her.

"You look tired, Honey. You can't do everything—including trying to take care of me. Please, I'm fine. Just upset, the same as you. Like you said, we'll find her tomorrow. And when we do, believe you me, I'm going to give her a sharp piece of my mind. That young lady is going to repent bitterly."

At that stern remark Bobby gave a little chuckle. "Yeah, sure. You'll be so happy to see her that all wrong-doing will cease to exist. I know you. A replica of your mother."

"Oh, Bobby, don't say that. Mama drove me and my sister crazy worrying and threatening punishment for our mistakes . . ."

"Which she never carried out."

"Well, we'll see tomorrow. Come on to bed now. I'm sleepy. And you need rest, too."

Bobby snapped off the lamp, rolled over to her, and slipping an arm around her waist, nestled to her back.

Karen stared into the blackness until her pupils adjusted to the semi-darkness of the summer night. Bobby's breathing became deep and regular. Karen wished she could fall asleep so quickly the way he always did.

Through the open window she could hear the gentle slapping of the water against the shore. She felt the chill of the night air against her cheeks. She had always loved the silence of cool wilderness nights. They made her feel part of something bigger and more solid, more permanent than city life. Her first night in the bush, on her honeymoon with Steve, she fell more in love with the magic and mystery of the forest night than she did with her bridegroom. But she had loved Steve . . . and most especially the child that was conceived on one of those first Canadian nights. Her eyelids became heavy and fell shut.

A sound. Her eyes blinked open. She listened. No, it wasn't coming through the window, it was in her head. Now she could hear it distinctly. The plaintive howl of wolves. Calling to one another. Calling to Meredith. Calling to her. She carefully lifted Bobby's arm off her waist and sat up. The sound continued.

This is what Meredith is hearing right now. She's near the wolves!

Karen felt her heart pounding against her chest. In spite of the night chill, she was perspiring. That same eerie feeling came over her—like the one she experienced on the Big Bear headed to Winnipeg. Only this time it brought assurance rather than panic.

She's not alone. And she's safe.

The sound stopped. The slap-slap of the lake resumed.

"Thank you, God, for this revelation," she whispered. She lay back down and continued silently half praying, half wishing.

Thank you for keeping her safe. I hope she's has found her Wolfie.

She closed her eyes and let sleep overtake her mind and body.

Who . . . could possibly be . . . with her . . . in the . . .wilderness . . .

* * *

Sometime during the few hours of semi-darkness of the Canadian night Karen awoke from a pleasant dream. She tried to reconstruct the sequence of the dream from the jigsaw-puzzle pieces of memory before they faded.

She was a little girl again, sitting on the living room floor in her family home in Spring Hill, South Carolina, stroking the sleak fur of Doojay, a lanky yellow tabby cat that was a vital part of the Kingsley family for nineteen years. She felt the rumble of his purring in her palm. "Karen, baby," her mother calling to her from the kitchen, calling her to supper. She uncrossed her legs, stood up and started in what she thought was the direction of the dining room. But the house was different, she no longer recognized the rooms, she didn't know which way to go. She looked left and right, but nothing seemed familiar. In a panic she whirled around and found Mama standing close behind her. She grabbed her mother around the thighs and, pressing her face hard against them, filled her nose, lungs, and heart with the warm, wonderful aroma of her mother's damp apron.

Karen had never forgotten the smell. She had cried many a childhood tear into that apron. It was a haven, a place that drained away all fretting, worrying, disappointment, and sadness. It made her childhood world a better place, a safe place. How many times in her adult life had she wished for the comfort of that apron. In her own kitchen, first in the house in Spring Hill with Steve then in Winnipeg with Bobby, she always wore an apron. Perhaps to offer the same hiding place to her own daughter. But she knew hers would never have the same healing power as her mother's. Besides, Meredith never seemed to need it. She couldn't remember a single time the child had flown to her in tears.

I wonder if she needs comforting now, if she needs my apron now. I've got to be warmer . . . and more nurturing toward her. She may seem mature and independent, but now I know she's still a child, a child capable of wrong decisions, a child who needs her mother more than ever.

Chapter Eight

Spring Hill, South Carolina, six years earlier.

"Have you had a mother-daughter talk about the 'birds and the bees' with Meredith?" Mrs. Kingsley rinsed the pot under the running hot water and handed it to Karen to dry.

"Mama, she's only ten years old. Isn't that a little young? To talk about those things? She thinks that boys are only good for climbing trees with or going fishing with. I don't think she's even close to, you know, that age yet."

Karen dried the boiler and hung it on the cookware rack above the kitchen counter, draped the dishcloth over the back of a chair at the breakfast table, and took a seat on the opposite chair facing the sink and her mother. How easily we fall back into the old routines in this house, Karen thought while her mother scoured the sink.

Mrs. Kingsley wiped her hands on her apron, removed the drying cloth from the chair back, folded it, and sat across from her daughter, holding the damp cloth like a handkerchief.

"Kids grow up much faster today. A friend told me that she heard about a girl who got pregnant at age ten. I guess she did more than climb trees and go fishing with some boy. If I were you, I wouldn't wait any longer. Besides, Meredith is smart and mature for her age."

"Of course you're right, Mama. I've just been putting it off until . . . until I saw some sign that she was about to start her periods."

"And by then it may be too late."

"To tell the truth, I'm not sure how to approach the subject. I'm afraid I'll confuse her or, worse, shock her."

Mrs. Kingsley reached across and patted Karen's hand. "You'll find the right words. There are probably some books at the library that can kinda guide you as to what to say and how to say it. But don't wait much longer, honey. You may even discover that she already knows just about everything."

"Oh, Mama, please. She's still a kid trying to imitate 'Uncle Bobby'."

"I think you've been hidden away in the Canadian woods too long. The world is changing. Not only here in the South, but everywhere.

Things are just not the same as they were when you and Katherine grew up."

"Did I hear my name mentioned?" The swinging door between the dining room and kitchen of the Kingsley home opened inward interjecting Karen's sister into the session of girl talk. She set the dinner casserole dish on the countertop.

"There's not much left. Do you want to save it?"

"Cover it with aluminum foil and put it in the refrigerator, dear. Your father sometimes raids the icebox at midnight. And he's especially fond of that chicken cordon bleu casserole. It'll disappear." Katherine did as she was told and went back through the swinging door.

Karen, Bobby, and Meredith, and Katherine and her husband Ted had enjoyed one of Mrs. Kingsley's home-cooked southern dinners. Following the family tradition, Katherine set the table before dinner and cleared it afterwards. Karen dried the dishes which her mother always washed by hand. She cherished those times working alone in the kitchen with her mother. It was a special time of sharing. But those times had become rare since she married Bobby and moved to Winnipeg, and tonight there were constant interruptions not only from Katherine but also from the men eager to help.

"Y'all just get in the way. Now go on out to the living room" Mrs. Kingsley gave her usual response to men in the kitchen. Karen knew her mother didn't appreciate husbands, son-in-laws or any male guests in the kitchen. That was women's private domain in her generation.

"I wish I could cook like you, Mama. And I wish I had even half of your wisdom."

"It's not wisdom, honey, it's plain common sense. Now let's go join the family in the living room. It's not often we get the opportunity to all be together. But don't you forget what I told you. Have that talk real soon."

"I will, Mama. I promise."

Karen finished a few tasks in the kitchen, but instead of going back to join the family in the living room, she left by the hall door and made her way up the dark wood staircase, allowing herself to enjoy the familiar feel of the newels, the smooth banister, and the scent of the aged wood of her childhood home. She had been born in this old-fashioned house on Oakmont Avenue in Spring Hill, and returned to live here for a while after she left Julliard—a homesick wannabe. She had lived here while she finished her Master of Music degree at Haywood

College until she met English Professor Steve Marsten and married him a week after graduating. Then after Steve's death, even though her parents had helped them build a dream home on a nearby lake, she had come back once again, this time to be comforted through the dark nights of grieving. Somehow in her heart this place would always be home. 248 Oakmont. 248 was her special number. It seemed to appear at uncanny moments in her life—on the digital alarm clock in the middle of the night, a seat number at a concert, a boarding pass, a door-prize stub. She never knew where or when it would appear, as if by divine design.

Her parents had kept her bedroom just as it was when she first left home for her undergraduate work at Converse College in Spartanburg. She opened the door and enveloped herself in its familiar intimacy. It was the constant in her ever-changing life. Walking over to the dresser she noticed the only addition to the room in eighteen years: a photograph of Steve and Bobby, each with an arm around the other's shoulder, Steve's wide grin and Bobby's shy half-smile. She had snapped the picture during that first trip to Poplar River on her honeymoon with Steve, when it seemed that life was full of good things and the promise of even better, that there could no evil befall them, that they would be young and carefree forever. The future was theirs for the taking. A jewel box next to the picture held the wedding ring she had never taken off until the day she accepted Bobby's proposal. She saved herself the pain of looking at it again.

She picked up the picture of Steve and Bobby. Stretching out on the bed, she placed the photo face-down over her heart and began to follow the threads of her life from that moment frozen in the picture. The tiny apartment she and Steve shared at first, walking distance to the college so Karen could have the car to drive to Oakmont to teach piano students in her parents home, and spend a little time—very little most days— practicing her own performance works and doing her technique studies. As much as she enjoyed teaching—well, most of her students were okay—and practicing her skills, she was always eager to get back to the three little rooms she shared with Steve. She loved that apartment where Meredith was born, in spite of the fact that she had endured a miscarriage of twin boys there a few years later. Even though they always considered the place temporary, it was still part of her, part of them, part of their engulfing romance that filled her heart for eight extraordinary years. Steve was sure to receive tenure—he had worked so hard for it—her career as a performing pianist was taking off, and Meredith was the single great joy of both their lives, in fact, of the lives of the whole family. Mama, Daddy, Katherine and Ted, who were childless, all adored her. She lit up the stars wherever she went.

Karen smiled as she thought of the beauty and tranquility of her first house—the lakeside home built on the lot which her mother and father had reserved for their own retirement home but instead had chosen to give it to her and Steve to build their dream home. And that's exactly what it was, nestled in red oaks and pines, with a screened porch overlooking the lake, a large living room to house the Steinway grand piano, and a study with floor-to-ceiling bookcases for Steve's class preparation and research. They had watched it become a reality board by board, brick by brick. It was their personal paradise, a place of work and play for both of them. Until that fateful evening of the lasagna. And though she still loved the place, she would never live there again. For a moment in her memory journey she felt the pain of Steve's death and a longing to go back to those halcyon days.

"No way. I know Bobby and I were destined to be together. He's more a part of me than anyone has ever been or ever will be," she told the photograph on her bosom. One day shortly after they were married, she had realized that his birthday, August 24, represented her magic number: 24 August—24-8.

She raised the picture enough to see Bobby's face. Joy ignited her heart and filled the deepest part of her. He was her soul mate, her husband, her helpmate, her lover, her best friend. She must be the luckiest woman in the world to be married to a man who was all these things.

She pictured their house in Winnipeg. A little two-story stucco charmer sandwiched on a postage-stamp sized lot on a typical Winnipeg street canopied by grandiose American elm trees. An alleyway ran parallel to the street behind the houses, providing entrance to individual garages. Between the garage and the house there was a portico that ran beside their garden. Above all her homes, Karen loved this simple place. Bobby had given her free rein to decorate it according to her whims. He had bought her a fine old Mason and Hamlin grand piano for the house, and a full Yamaha keyboard to take to the wilderness lodge. The architectural design was quaint, reminding her of an early English farm house, with a little gable over the front door. The interior was compact but full of unusual little nooks and crannies. So different from this rambling old southern home of her young years.

The last leg of her journey through her various dwelling places—Baldwin Lake Lodge—was interrupted by a knock on the door.

"Karen? Are you asleep?" The door opened a crack. "Wake up, Sweetie, it's time to put Meredith to bed. Remember, we're leaving early tomorrow morning. Have to be at the airport by 7:30."

"Come on in, Bobby. I wasn't asleep, just reminiscing about things—and realizing for the umpteenth million time how much I love you."

* * *

"Mama, I know how babies are made. The older kids that take sex education classes tell us everything. About eggs and sperm and all that. And about the diseases you can get."

Karen had followed her mother's advice and broached the subject of sex with her daughter shortly after the visit to Spring Hill.

"Well, okay. But biology isn't all I wanted us to discuss. It's important to know about feelings—about love. One day you will meet a boy that is very special to you, not only for going fishing, climbing trees, and other fun things like that. I mean he will affect you—mentally and physically. You will feel something special in your heart as well as in your body. Over time, if all goes well between the two of you, the feeling will develop into love." Karen took a deep breath before continuing. "You see, real love is a rich and beautiful thing. It's a combination of body, mind, and heart. And all three must be in perfect accord. The beginning of it can be very powerful. Do you understand?"

"I understand, but I don't think I've ever had that feeling."

"Of course you haven't, sugar baby. You're too young yet. But soon your body will began preparing you physically for experiencing all those feelings, getting you ready so that when the time comes you will have children."

"You mean I will get my monthly periods."

"That's exactly what I mean. So you know about that, too?"

"Then will I have those feelings?"

"Well, you see," Karen swallowed. "Sometimes we get the physical feeling before we find the special person who touches our heart and mind. That's when we can get into trouble. If we're only listening to our body, doing what it tells us to do, then we might want to have . . .uh . . . sexual relations with someone who is not the right one. The best thing to

do is wait to be intimate with that special person. And it usually takes a long time to know for sure that someone you meet is the right one, the special one."

"I know, Mama. Then you get married."

Karen took her daughter in her arms. "Yes, then you get married."

"Like you and Uncle Bobby. He's your special one."

"You are so smart, darling! I hope you will always remember this talk with your mother."

"I will, Mama. Forever."

Karen gave Meredith a loud, happy kiss of relief.

Chapter Nine

Where the heck is Travis? Supposed to be here at nine, and it's going on ten. If it weren't for the money, I'd be long gone.

Manny had been nursing his beer for a half an hour. Sitting at the bar in McGill's Tavern on Portage Road, he had glanced at his watch a dozen times. He took another sip from his glass of LaBatt's Blue and looked at his watch again.

That guy is bad news. Always operates a little the other side of the law. I oughta get out of here right now. But . . . to make a thousand bucks in two days, I'd like to hear what he has to say.

"Hey, Manny, how's Melissa?" Buddy, the owner, was tending bar tonight.

"About the same, Bud. She's taking regular dialysis treatments, but she really needs that operation. She's on the waiting list for a kidney donor, but you know it's gotta be compatible. Mine's not."

"Any luck landing a job?"

"Nothing. I've fallen way behind on mortgage payments. Times are pretty hard."

"You think you might lose the house?"

"Looks that way, if things don't change in a hurry. Melissa doesn't know. She's got enough on her right now."

"Maybe I ought to put a little donation jar out on the bar."

"By the time we raised enough, the whole lot of us would be pushing up daisies." He gulped down the last of his beer.

"Tough situation, Man. Want another one?" He gestured toward Manny's empty glass. "It's on the house. Sorry. No pun intended."

Manny nodded. A somebody-done-somebody-wrong song started playing on the juke box. Country music always comforted Manny. Songs with a twangy sadness in the voice and those that expressed determination to get even made him feel he wasn't the only one in the world with problems. He sipped his second beer and listened to the song and to the clack of billiard balls in the far corner of the tavern.

"Sorry I'm late, Man. Had a little business to take care of." Travis settled his boney bottom on the stool next to Manny. His clothes were seedy and gave off a sour odor.

"Yeah? Like evading the local authorities?"

"Shut up and listen. We're going hunting."

"Hunting? For what?"

"Shut up, I said. We're gonna bag a moose, well, at least the head."

"I don't know anything about moose hunting."

"I'll take care of the hunting. All you have to do is carry a rifle, a saw, and a plastic bag."

"A saw?"

"I do the shooting, you do the sawing and hauling. I know you're strong 'cause you've worked as a logger. Or had you rather use an axe?"

Manny pushed his glass away, put his elbows on the bar, and cradled his face in his palms. He sat. Travis began drumming his fingers on the bar.

"It's a lot of money, quickest you'll ever make. A month or so ago I made over five k off a bear. All I had to carry out was a couple of paws and the gall bladder. The Chinese are crazy about that stuff. Make medicine out of it. Pay a lot for it."

"You S.O.B., you know you've got me between a rock and a hard place."

"Think of it as a camping trip."

Manny took a deep breath. "Yeah. Sure."

"The head is worth a lot more than just the rack. The whole head and part of the neck. No way the two of us could haul out the whole body. Wish we could, though. That'd put us on easy street."

Travis twisted on the bar stool and looked around as if casing the room then turned back to Manny.

"As soon as all the arrangements are made, I'll get back to you with the details. And you'll keep your mouth shut, right?"

He slipped his thin frame off the stool and out the door.

Manny stared at the countertop.

Buddy came over, drying a martini glass with a white cloth. He leaned toward Manny and spoke in a low voice. "Don't have anything to do with him, Man. He's trouble. Big trouble."

"I know." Manny stood up, stuffed a dollar bill in the tip jar at the end of the counter, and stepped out into the night. Crossing the parking lot, he wondered what in the world he would tell Melissa. When he reached the door of his pick-up, he stopped.

Saw the head off a moose, let the blood drain out, put the thing in a bag, and drag it through the bush. I must be out of my mind. The whole business is disgusting and probably illegal. What if we're caught? Melissa would never survive. I don't see how I can do it. But, God, I need the money.

He unlocked the truck, slid into the driver's seat, and put the key into the ignition. He clasped his hands at the top of the steering wheel and leaned his forehead against his knuckles. *I have to do it. But just this once. For Melissa.*

* * *

Manny sat in the back of the float plane trying to hear what Travis and the pilot were saying, but the engine noise was deafening. He settled back to gaze at the land and water configurations beneath him. Lakes and streams, unspoiled by human invasion, sprawled out in natures capricious patterns. Some resembled animals—a snail, a beaver, a rat. Others suggested inanimate forms—a cart, a banjo, an hourglass—only not as symmetrical. Through the translucence of shallow water he could discern rocky shelves, boulders and submerged trees. A rainbow of colors displayed the varied depths from the yellow-green of the shallowest to the blue-black of the deep. The spectrum absorbed his attention and, at least for a while, eased his spirit.

The motor slowed, the plane banked and descended. Manny had no idea what lake they were landing on, but he didn't care. He just wanted this ordeal over with, done, and forgotten. The pilot killed the motor and let the plane drift into shallow water close to the shore. Travis opened his door and stepped onto a float. Pressing his forehead against the back window, Manny peered down and watched him release a canoe that was tied to the struts. The pilot leaned around toward Manny.

"Okay, pal. You can get out now and into the canoe. But watch your step."

Manny did watch each step. He was already taking a chance dealing with Travis. He didn't want any mishaps. Once safely seated in the canoe, he looked around. The lake was wide, wider than he had expected, and lay serene, glistening with the soft tangerine and blue of the sunrise. A thin nocturnal mist still lingered over the tops of the tall spruce trees. The aroma of balsam wafted in the air. The hush of the wilderness pressed hard on Manny's conscience. He was an intruder, an intruder who was about to become an assassin, a mutilator. And it was too late to back out now.

Travis stood in the canoe catching the gear tossed down from the pilot. Manny wondered how he kept his balance. Including the backpacks, rifles, and a duffle bag, the little canoe was fully loaded and sat low in the water.

"Pick up a paddle, Man. You gotta earn your keep," Travis spoke with his usual cavalier attitude and low-life grin. Manny did as told. Travis swiveled the canoe around, placing himself in front. He seemed to know where he was headed. Manny was thankful for that.

The pilot cranked up the plane engine. Manny turned to watch him taxi out to deep water for take-off. A flood of anxiety gripped his chest and spread into his abdomen and down through his legs. He had abandoned himself to a menacing fate over which he no longer had any control.

"Paddle, Man! And keep your eye on the shoreline. We might get lucky and spot a bear or maybe a wolf. If you do, shoot the sucker."

"I thought we came for a moose. How could we keep a bear or a wolf while hunting a moose?"

"Who said anything about keeping him? You're right. We're after a moose, a big bull moose. But nothing wrong with enjoying a little sport shooting while we're here."

Manny gritted his teeth and sliced into the water with his paddle. They slipped along the shoreline in a silence broken occasionally by the high-pitched squeal of a bald eagle or the raucous squawking vee of Canada geese in flight.

When Melissa gets well and I find a job, we're going to spend some time in nature. Go camping, fishing, boating. It'll be good for both of us.

Manny pictured the two of them out on a lake like this one. Away from civilization. She would be smiling, happy, healthy. No more dialysis, no more pills, no more fear or financial woes. He was beginning to feel hopeful that they would get their old life back, only with more time together, more love demonstrated, more appreciation for the little things, the little moments in life.

I'll start going to church with her when she gets able. She'll be real happy about that.

"Head in toward that cove over there." Travis pointed to a tangle of trees beyond which the shoreline sagged in. They angled in, nosing the front of the canoe partially onto the shore with the paddles. Travis hopped out, Manny followed. They pulled the canoe completely out of the water. Before Travis started unloading he fished around in the duffle bag.

"Here's what you'll need." He held up two large pieces of folded material, one of heavy burlap-type cloth, and one of dark green plastic.

"What's this?"

"What do you think it is? It's the game bags, you moron. For the trophy. Put it in the plastic one first, then this one."

"Then what?"

"Jeez, are you stupid? You carry it—or drag it—back to the pick-up spot. I thought you had enough brains to do this, but I can see I was wrong." He stuffed the game bags back into the duffle, pulled two rifles from the hull of the canoe, and laid them on a flat lichen-covered rock. "I sure hope you know how to use one of these."

"Yeah, they taught us in the Army."

Travis finished unloading the gear, tossing onto the ground two full backpacks, each with a sleeping bag and tightly-rolled hiker's mat secured to the bottom. A saw handle stuck out of the top of one.

"Now help me get the boat up into the bushes. Don't want any freakin' fishermen helping themselves to our transportation." He lifted one end of the canoe. Manny lifted the other. "Coming in we spotted a floatplane not too far from here. Pilot said it was probably just some guys out to fish the lake for the day. There ain't no lodges or outposts on this lake, nowhere near it. They'd better not be here after my moose."

"Could that mean trouble?"

"Naw, I don't think so, but you never know."

That sick grin again.

Travis strapped on a backpack and grabbed one of the rifles.

"Annie get your gun, or should I say *Mannie* get your gun." He snorted at his own humor, nodded toward the mossy rock, turned his back, and started into the bush.

"Hey, wait a minute," Manny called after him. "How will they know when to pick us up?"

Travis answered without stopping or turning around.

"We've got two full days and two full nights. That's all. The time's all set. So there can't be any screw-ups. Got it?"

Manny took a deep breath and blew it out hard. He strapped on the backpack, shouldered the rifle, grabbed the duffle with the saw and followed his leader into a dark, ominous forest.

* * *

"How long do we have to wait?" Manny's legs were tired. They had walked from the canoe that delivered them to this God-forsaken place, waded through mushy-bottomed lowlands, then hiked non-stop up a trail that was not fit for man nor beast, at least not for man. There had been precious few rest stops, included one for lunch that didn't even give Manny time to finish his cheese sandwich and Coke. They had located the stream where Travis on his bear-poaching trip had seen a large moose feeding. They unrolled their lightweight mats and sleeping bags and slept until daybreak. Now they were waiting for the "big bull" to put in his morning appearance. Manny sat cross-legged on a patch of moss trying to rub the cramps out of his calves.

"Till he gets here."

"My feet and legs are all knotted up."

"Just think of the money and stop your belly-aching." Travis cleared his throat and spat to one side.

After a long wait in silence, Manny heard movement in the brush.

"It's him, Man. Don't move."

Travis slowly raised himself into position, pointing the rifle toward the stream.

"Damn! He's big. Just like I remember," he whispered.

Manny wanted to get a look at the creature. He unfolded his legs and tried to stand but his muscles gave way. He fell against Travis just as the shot was fired.

"You stupid fool! You made me miss him. I oughta shoot *you*."

The moose had retreated into the woods at full speed. Travis took off after him, leaving Manny with all the gear. He rolled up the mats and sleeping bags, fastened them to the backpacks, slung one over each shoulder, and picked up his rifle and the duffle. He tried to run after Travis but couldn't. Too much weight. And his legs were still cramped.

We've gotta get this moose. Then we can go home as soon as they fly in to get us.

Loaded with all the gear, Manny gathered his courage and hobbled after Travis and the big bull moose.

* * *

When he caught up with Travis, his partner was sitting with his back against a tree, swigging from a flask.

"Should you be drinking now? What if we spot the moose again?"

"Calms me down. My hands will be steadier when I pull the trigger.

You want a belt?"

Manny shook his head. "I need all my wits about me to survive out here."

"Good. I only brought enough for me." He took another sip, screwed the cap on and shoved the flask into a pocket of his hunting vest.

"Where'd the moose go?" Manny asked.

Travis looked up and squinted at him. "He went to a movie. What the hell do you mean 'where'd the moose go?' He went into the woods, you idiot."

Manny dropped all the baggage beside Travis.

"What do we do now?"

"I've got just the thing that will get him back." He reached into the duffle and pulled out something that resembled a large ice cream cone. "This'll bring him running."

"What is that?"

"This here's a gen-u-wine Ojibwe moose caller. Made out of birch bark and sewed up with spruce root. It imitates the sound of a cow in heat."

"I bet that's beautiful."

"It is to the bull, I guarantee you. This time when he shows up, keep your distance and keep still. Don't move a friggin' muscle. Don't even breathe. You scare him off again and your head will be the trophy hanging in a lodge dining room."

Manny found his own tree to lean against and sat his baggage down beside him.

If I never see Travis again in my life, it'll be too soon. He thought about Melissa for the first time since they entered the bush. He had decided not to deceive her. He didn't tell her anything before he left, just that he had a part-time job that would take him away for a few days.

"Two or three days? Where are you going? What kind of job? Manny, I don't want you to get in trouble. Tell me what this is all about."

"I will when I get back. Just trust me. It'll be okay."

"What if they find a kidney while you're gone?"

"Buddy will take you to the hospital, and I'll be there as soon as I can."

"Manny, please don't leave me here alone. Please don't do this. I don't feel right about it. Besides, I need you with me."

She had made it doubly hard for him to show up the next day to meet Travis. He wished now he had stayed home. He surely could have found a better way to make money.

If I hadn't messed up that shot, the whole ordeal would be over by now.

Uh-ahn-n-n-nh. The loud guttural sound scared Manny half out of his wits. Travis was blowing the moose caller. They waited. He blew again. They waited again. Every few minutes a phony female moose called out for a lover then waited for one to show up.

"Okay. Here's what we're going to do—and this always works. We're going to use our flashlights and hunt the moose after dark. I know he's around, he's heard the female calling, and he wants to come looking for her, but he knows we're here. He'll feel safe and more like humpin' after dark. Right now I'm hungry. Let's dig out some grub."

Travis opened his backpack. They ate cans of deviled ham and green peas, cold—a fire would deter the moose, according to Travis.

"This canned stuff is giving me indigestion." Manny wiped his camping fork off, flipped it back up into the Swiss Army Knife, and buttoned it into the breast pocket of his lumberjack shirt.

"I guess you just don't have a stomach for this sort of thing," Travis quipped and laughed so hard at his own wit that food spurted out of his mouth.

"You wanna play the part of the moose bitch?" With an ironic smirk on his face, he offered Manny the caller. "Be my guest."

Manny looked away. *The guy is actually enjoying himself.*

After what seemed like eons of time and a billion moose calls, Travis decided it was nap time. He took another few swigs from the flask and settled back against his tree. "What kinda name is 'Manny' anyway? Is that a nickname ? Isn't it short for a Spic name? Manello, or something like that?"

"No."

"Well, it's a real peculiar name."

Manny began loosening the laces of his work boots. "It's actually from the Bible—Emmanuel. According to my mother it means 'God with us.' She and my father had about given up hope of having a child. She was in her late thirties when she finally got pregnant. They thought it was a gift from God, so that's why they picked that name. You know there's a story in the Bible about an older woman—Abraham's wife, I think— who was visited by angels and had a baby late in life. That sound familiar?"

He glanced up at Travis. His head had fallen to one side, eyes closed, jaw hanging. *The alcohol. And probably my bible story. I'd better get some sleep, too.* He curled into a fetal position, but Travis' snoring and his own apprehension kept him awake. At least his legs felt better. He found some consolation in visualizing life with Melissa after her recovery when he would be working and they could once again be happy doing things together. It helped pass the time.

Just as Manny was finally dozing off, Travis jumped to his feet. "He's back!"

In the dimness of the summer night Manny could see the outline of a large bull standing not more that five or six meters from them. Without taking his eyes off the moose, he hurriedly retied his shoe laces.

"Grab the flashlight, Man. Shine it directly in his eyes." Travis' words were low and rapid. Manny did as he was told. He moved around, aiming the beam at the animal until he had it pointing at the face. The moose stood perfectly still. Travis had plenty of time to take precise aim. He fired one shot. The moose fell. It struggled, flailing its legs and twisting its massive body trying to get on its feet again. Manny shut off the flashlight and stood in the dark until the struggle ended.

"As soon as it gets daylight, you can saw off the trophy," Travis said then unscrewed the cap of his flask. "Damn beast didn't utter a sound, did he?"

Chapter Ten

They had traveled only a short time through the bush when Meredith spotted water straight ahead.

"What lake is that?" she called out to Mark who was leading the way.

"The same one you landed on. Just farther north"

"It's really close to your camp, then."

"Yeah. I do a lot of fishing. Fish is my main staple."

They reached the shore. "I keep my boat here," Mark explained. "For fishing and exploring."

Meredith noticed a small motor boat pulled up on the bank.

"That it?" she nodded in that direction.

"Yep. All nine horsepower."

"I think a canoe would be more traditional."

"Another concession," Mark grinned.

She checked out the boat and found a couple of fishing rods and a tackle box stored inside. "More concessions?"

"You're starting to make me feel guilty!"

"Why did we come here? Are we going to use the boat for transportation?"

"The path that leads up to where the wolves hang out starts from here—if you can call it a path. It gets pretty rough. Are you up for it?"

"That's what I came for."

"Okay. Stay close to me and do what I do. It's quite a trek."

"Aye, aye, sir," Meredith saluted. She was starting to feel less nervous and enjoy this. A good-looking guy leading her to Wolfie, and the weather was promising to be warm enough and dry.

The northward path was easy to travel at first, except for a few low jack pine branches they had to duck and blueberry bushes that swiped them on both sides, the going was not too bad—until they came to a ravine. Mark stopped.

"What now?" she asked, looking down at the steep incline.

"The animals go down one side and up the other. And we could do that, too. But I have a way to swing across."

Mark walked to a large blue spruce and produced a long, heavy rope. Tied to a sturdy-looking branch, it had a loop in the middle and one at the bottom. "What you do is grab the upper loop with one hand and hold the rope with the other. Put a foot in the lower loop—like this." He demonstrated the proper swinging position, backed up a few steps, and, with a running start, did a pendulum swing over the crevasse, hopped off on the other side, but held on to the rope.

"It's easy. Watch again." He swung back across.

"You must be Tarzan."

"Go ahead. Give it a try. Get off on the other side. The worst you could do is fall and break a leg or two." He handed her the rope.

Meredith's mouth fell open. "O---kay. Uh, how good are you at setting broken bones?" She passed Mark the rifle, took the rope, and, duplicating his running start, stuck her right foot in the loop and swung across the ravine. With eyes riveted on Mark's landing spot on the other side, she prayed to dismount on *terra firma* before the backswing could take her out again. She did it. *Thank you, Jesus!*

Mark applauded.

"Good girl! Me Tarzan, you Jane. Now toss the rope back to me." Mark followed his protégé, the rifle strapped to his shoulder along with the beaded bag.

With the swing-line secured to a tree on the far side, the journey toward the wolves continued.

The footing here was more difficult. Fallen limbs and deep holes hid under a thick bed of leaves. The underbrush was denser, bushes were fuller, and branches were lower. They had to walk hunched over most of the time. Meredith had to concentrate on each step.

"Do you need to rest a little?" Mark asked after a long, silent trek.

"Only if you do." Meredith was determined to prove her woodsmanship.

"I think we could use a break."

A fallen white pine served as table and chairs. Mark opened his bag and retrieved a breadcake with splotchy burns, evidence that it had been cooked over an open fire. As he did, a red fox dashed by.

"Here. This'll give you a boost." He broke the bread and handed half to Meredith.

But before she could take her first bite of the physical and moral booster, she noticed that Mark was focused on something behind her. His pupils widened. He spoke one word firmly and clearly.

"Bear."

She turned her head to glance over shoulder. A large brownish-red bear stood less than ten feet behind her, watching them.

"Don't move. But look for a tree you can climb if necessary." Mark spoke calmly.

He stood up. With a forceful tone he directed some Ojibwe words at the bruin. No one moved. Not Meredith, not Mark, not the bear. Meredith could feel her body trembling, inside and out. Mark took a step forward, squared his shoulders, and repeated the words, louder this time. Out of the corner of her eye Meredith could see the bear swinging his head from side to side. His snorting nearly stopped her heart. Bobby stood his ground, staring directly at the bear. It was a standoff. After what seemed like an eternity of snorting, pawing the ground, and head-swinging, the bear turned and walked away, making a noise that sounded like teeth clacking. Mark didn't move for a minute or two. Finally he let out a long breath of relief.

"I think it's okay now. He's gone. All five-hundred pounds of the brute."

Meredith's breathing was shallow and fast with fear. It took her a minute to regain control enough to speak.

"Oh my God, Mark! I didn't even hear him come up, did you?"

"They're good at coming through the bush without making any noise, in spite of their tonnage. And he was big, bigger than your average black bear."

"But he wasn't black."

"There are different colorations of the species 'black bear.' Cinnamon is one. They're usually larger than the black ones, but not aggressive. I've had a number of bear encounters without any problem. They're more afraid of us than we are of them. I bank on that."

"What was that strange clacking noise he made?"

"I think when he gets a little nervous, he snaps his teeth together, fast. He's just trying to fake being brave. I was sort of faking it, too."

Meredith had held on to her piece of bread. She tried to take a bite, but her hands were still shaking. Mark picked up the rifle with one hand and remained standing while he ate his bread with the other.

Meredith finally managed to chew and swallow. "Do you think he'll come back?"

"Not today."

"Do you think he was after our food?"

"No, probably that fox. And we interrupted the chase. I'm sure he wasn't too happy about that. The bear, that is. The fox is probably grateful to us."

"You're so calm in the face of danger. I'm amazed."

"I'm amazed that you didn't scream or run."

"How could I? I was so frozen with fear that I couldn't move or utter a sound." She immediately regretted admitting her lack of *sang froid* to her companion. "Teach me those words and I'll say them to the next bear we meet up with." *I really wish I had eyes in the back of my head. I don't want to be surprised again,* she admitted to herself.

"I doubt we'll see another. They are rather scarce up here in wolf territory."

The bear question settled and the bread eaten, Meredith and Mark resumed their quest for the wolf pack. Her earlier carefree attitude had dissipated with the stealthy appearance of Bruno. She was all caution, attuning her ears and eyes to the dangers lurking in the boreal forest.

* * *

"What's that sound? Do you hear it, off in the distance?" Meredith asked.
It's kind of a hiss and kind of a roar."

Mark stopped to listen. "I think you mean the waterfall. You wanna see it?"

"If it's not too far off the wolf trail."

"It's not far. Don't worry. I know very well how to get there and back. It's my shower."

"And I guess the lake is your bathtub."

Mark smiled.

He has such a great smile, Meredith noted. In fact, she had been adding up a number of things about Mark that she admired, not the least of which was his mastery of the bear. And, of course, the fact that he was tall, dark, and handsome had not escaped her notice, nor had his well-defined muscles. All of these attributes were creating quite a stir in Meredith's mind, heart, and body. One thing she knew for sure—she wanted to be with him, and not just for protection and the feeling of security he gave her. There were other feelings, too. New feelings that she didn't understand. Strange and wonderful feelings.

"We have to crisscross the stream. Be careful. Walk along the log if you don't want to get your feet wet." They had reached a shallow flow of water over which someone—presumably Mark—had thrown a tree trunk. Mark started across then turned back to Meredith.

"Maybe you'd better give me your hand."

With one hand secure in Mark's firm grip, she stretched the other out to sustain her balance. She didn't have much practice walking on logs. In spite of her poised, well-placed steps, one wobble almost sent both of them into the water.

"There we are, 'high and dry' on the other side." Mark quipped, releasing her hand.

"I thought for a second we were going to be 'low and wet.'"

"You're a good kid."

I think he likes my humor, but does he really think of me as a 'kid'?

Judging from the sound of rushing water, Meredith knew the waterfall was close by. Farther along, the path crossed back over the brook where there were rocks to use as stepping stones. They followed the water's edge upstream. In only a few minutes they reached the waterfall. It wasn't very wide or powerful this late in the summer, but its gushing sound filled the silence of the woods.

"It's not as big as I thought, but it is beautiful," Meredith said.

"In the spring, with all the melting snow and ice, it's much bigger—and a lot louder, with a strong current."

They watched the cascading waters in silence for a few moments.

"Mni-ha ha," Mark said.

"What?"

"Mni-ha ha. Ojibwe for 'waterfall.'"

"Knee-haw-haw?"

"Not exactly, but close. It's almost the same as in Longfellow's poem about Hiawatha."

"Oh, I know now! We have always said it like 'minnie ha-ha.' And that means 'waterfall'? My first Ojibwe word."

"I can teach you a lot more, if you like."

"I'd like that." With that response strange sensations surged in her body and soul. She had a fleeting vision of the two of them, living together in the forest, speaking to each other in Ojibwe. Then she remembered the bear and came back to reality.

They continued to admire the mni-ha ha. Another vision, this one more vivid and not so brief. Meredith pictured Mark naked under the flood, his face upturned, letting the falling water flow through his long dark hair, roll over his shoulders and down his muscular back and legs.

"If you want to take a shower, I'll discretely turn my back. But I warn you, the water is really cold," Mark offered.

"I would *love* a shower!" She really didn't want to get wet, but she couldn't pass up this perfect opportunity to demonstrate her outdoorsmanship.

"Then, by all means, go ahead." Mark sat down on a boulder with his back to her.

Meredith quickly shed her clothes and, careful not to lose her balance again, stepped into the water and stood under the icy falls.

"Wow! It *is* cold! But it feels great." She tried to keep her hair as dry as possible. With no towel or electric hairdryer, she would have a mass of tight wet curls the rest of the day—or until she could get back to civilization.

"Okay, what do I dry off with?"

"The air."

"You're kidding. I'm freezing!"

"Here, take my jacket and wear it until you're dry enough to put your clothes back on." He pulled the deerskin jacket off and passed it around behind his back. "You did take your clothes off, didn't you?"

"I always take showers fully clothed, don't you?" Although Meredith couldn't see it, she knew he was smiling that devastating smile once again.

The jacket still held his warmth and aroma. Slipping it over her bare skin evoked more strange sensations. Powerful ones that warmed her inside as well as out and made her feel dizzy.

"While you're dealing with clothing, I'll get lunch ready. The cold water always makes me hungry. Besides, I'm always hungry in the bush."

"You brought lunch?" Meredith slipped on panties, hooked her bra and pulled on her jeans and two sweaters. Sitting on a rock slab, she donned her socks then laced up her boots. Hoping to strike an alluring pose, she stood, picked up her jacket, hooked it on two fingers, and slung it over a shoulder. With the other hand she fluffed her hair as best she could.

Mark was taking some items out of his beaded bag, still with his back to her.

"You can turn around now."

Mark swiveled to face her. Slowly but surely the smile returned.

"You look beautiful—beautifully clean and refreshed."

His words and the look on his face heated her blood more than any jacket or coat ever could. She made a mental video of the moment: Mark sitting on the boulder beside the stream gazing at her, the sound of the waterfall drowned out by the pounding of her heart. She would replay the video a thousand times in her head.

* * *

They had no trouble making it back to the path. In fact, Mark took a different route that put them farther up the trail toward the wolves, and there was no need to cross the stream again. At first Mark walked ahead of her as he had done since they started out, pausing occasionally to look back just to make sure she was keeping up. After a while he stopped and waited for her to reach him. Without saying a word, he took her hand, smiled, and continued along the path holding her close behind him.

The feel of his hand clasping hers filled her heart with a wild joy— one she had never known before. It was frightening, being overwhelmed by such powerful and contrasting emotions one after another. The scare of the storm and forced landing, the panic at being lost in the wilderness, the fear during the bear episode alternated with the sound sleep on his bearskin pallet, the exchange of witty remarks and gentle teasing, the pleasure of his warm jacket against her skin, now his hand in hers. She swallowed hard, blinked forcibly, and tried to concentrate on her footing.

"We're almost there," he said.

"Where the wolves are?"

"And maybe your Wolfie."

Meredith felt a rush of anticipation. *I'm going to see Wolfie again, I just know it. And he is all right. I hope he remembers me.* She walked with renewed spirit.

Two minutes later Mark stopped dead in his tracks, dropped her hand. Meredith stepped up to his side and gasped at a scene more horrible than anything she could ever have imagined. She brought both hands to her mouth and nose in a gasp of horror and held them there to block out the stench. The head of the moose was gone, severed at the base of the neck. Flies swarmed over the raw flesh. Blood saturated the ground around the animal. And there were footprints in the blood-soaked earth—human footprints.

"Native Americans?" Meredith was the first to speak, forgetting that she was addressing one.

Mark's eyes narrowed. "No. We hunt moose for food, not for trophies. We would never do this. We honor animals in life and in death."

She could tell by the sound of his voice and the look on his face that he was both saddened and angered by what he must view as an unpardonable act of transgression.

"Poachers. A few taxidermists deal with poachers. Sell the mounted heads to adorn the walls of restaurants or pool halls . . . or some rich guy's den. This was an older bull moose. Must've had a nice rack." Mark paused, then spoke as if whispering to himself. "I consider him my elder brother."

He walked all the way around the huge cadaver, stopping here and there for a close look. "Just one bullet wound. They probably shot him last night. Used a light to blind him then fired at the reflecting eyes. It's a sure kill, but an illegal one." He turned and glanced at the brush surrounding them.

"They may be carrying the trophy back along the path we originally took. We could have met up with them if we hadn't veered off to see the waterfall." Mark hesitated. "Or they may be going after more trophies— a bear or a wolf."

Meredith shuddered. *Wolfie. What if they get Wolfie.* She tightened her jaw and clenched her teeth.

"Is there anything we can do to stop them?"

"Nothing short of trying to find out who they are and reporting them to the Conservation Office or the police. By then they'll be long gone."

"The Conservation Office?"

"They issue licenses and regulate hunting. In cases of poaching, enforcement officers work with the Royal Canadian Mounted Police. They would arrest these guys—if they ever find them. Not too long ago they caught a couple of guys in this same area poaching bear for their paws and gall bladders."

"What in the world were they going to do with them?"

"Certain bear parts bring a high price on the black market. They're used a lot in the far east for medicine."

"It's hard to believe anyone could be so cruel. So what are we going to do?"

"We're going to continue to search for your wolf. It's too late to help this old fellow. It could be dangerous for us to get involved. Sorry you had to see this."

He walked to the other side of the mutilated corpse opposite Meredith, lowered his head and began a soft chant in his native language. Meredith bowed her head, too. *It must be some kind of prayer for the moose.* She respected the moment in silence. The long notes lingered above the moose's body, enveloping it in sacredness and sorrow, creating a temple in the midst of the wilderness. Meredith's own heart joined in. *Please, Dear God, receive into your kingdom the spirit of this moose which you formed so beautifully. Forgive those who destroyed him and bless those who honor him. Amen.*

The chant ended. Mark looked across the body at his traveling companion.

"Let's go find Wolfie, Miss Mni-ha ha. Their rendez-vous spot is not far."

"What if we should encounter the poachers?"

"We won't. In any case, let me worry about that." He was carrying the rifle.

Keeping her distance she went around the moose remains to join hands with Mark and continue the incredible journey.

The trail narrowed and the terrain became more difficult to traverse. Meredith was beginning to tire and was about to ask Mark for a short break when he set down the rifle and his bag.

"Okay. I think we'll camp here for the night. The wolf pack will rendez-vous over there." He pointed to a small elevation about one hundred meters to the west. The sun was low behind the hill.

"We should be able to see them from here. We'll definitely hear them."

"I thought this was a day trip. I didn't know we were going to camp out."

"It's a full day's hike from my place, if you include a shower. Don't worry. I'll provide us with food and a little shelter."

Meredith zipped up her jacket against the growing chill of the evening air.

"Here's a good spot for our fire." He selected a fire site in front of a little shelf of land with a concave curve to it.

"The wall will reflect the fire and project more heat. Then we can sleep nestled up against the warm bank."

"That's sounds good. I am a bit tired—and hungry."

"Help me scout around for kindling and dry wood. Then we can eat by the fire."

Mark had a blaze going within minutes. Meredith sat down cross-legged between the bank and the fire. Mark settled beside her, opened his bag, and handed her a piece of smoked meat.

"That looks good." She tore off a bite of the meat. "Ummmm. Beaver meat?"

"I hate to tell you. It's moose."

She stopped chewing. The piece of meat seemed to grow larger in her mouth and her stomach did a flip.

"It is really tasty. Not gamey like venison. True hunters, the ones I respect, are after the meat, not a trophy," Mark said, chewing as he spoke.

Once she forced herself to swallow, Meredith could agree with him. It was tasty and tender.

"I do like it. No wonder it is a favorite meat among First Nations people," she declared and took another bite, making a concerted effort not to envision the headless cadaver.

Mark took out a small bottle of liquid and gave it to her. "It's berry juice. It'll help you digest the meat while it slakes your thirst."

She took a sip. "Whoa! That's a little too bitter for me."

Mark laughed. "It was for me, too, at first. But you'll get used to it."

I'll get used to it? Does that mean he thinks I'll be eating and drinking like he does in the bush? It's like I've already become part of his wilderness lifestyle. Not that I would mind . . . someday.

"Can I ask you something?" Meredith swallowed another mouthful of meat then took a sip of the juice, grimacing as the bitter liquid roughed her tongue.

"Sure. Anything."

"Your name is Mark, and your grandfather is Tom. Those are anglo names. Don't you have another name? I mean, one in your Indian language—one that has special meaning?"

"You're absolutely right. I do have an Ojibwe name. My grandparents found it unusual that, as a toddler, I would often look at the sky, point to birds, clouds, the moon, the stars, anything I saw up there. One day, after a heavy morning shower, the sun came out and formed a very distinct rainbow that arched across the heavens. Apparently when I saw it I became ecstatic with joy, jumping up and down and screaming in delight. So they named me *nagweyaab*—rainbow."

"Nawg-way-yob?"

"That's pretty close. Sometimes, at the waterfall, when the sun is shining just right, you can see a rainbow in the falling waters. Then, mni-ha-ha and nagweyaab are together." The smile again.

Mark stood. "I'll be right back."

He walked away, leaving Meredith to tend the fire and to ponder the implication in Mark's last words. He walked toward a tall white spruce, lifted something from its lower branches, and returned.

"Here's a tarpaulin we can use to cover up with. I keep it in the area for the times I sleep here."

"You sleep here?"

"I have a trap line not far from here that I like to check early in the mornings. Catch mostly rabbit. Sometimes a marten or a fox." Mark spread the tarp over the bank behind the fire. "There. It'll get nice and warm. I'll try to keep the fire going throughout the night so you won't get cold and so we won't have any unwanted furry visitors. I hope you're not still hungry."

"No, I'm fine." A vision of the head-swinging bear danced for a moment in her mind. She quickly deleted it. "But I am ready for some sleepy-time."

"So am I."

Mark stretched out under the tarp and propped himself up on one elbow. He patted the tarp in a motion that meant for Meredith to join him. She sat beside him on top of the cover with her arms wrapped around her knees.

"It's kinda chilly," she said.

"We'll have to depend on each other for more warmth," Mark said. "The fire won't be quite enough." He sat up, took her arm, and turned her toward him. She complied by swiveling around on one hip. His face was a breath away from hers.

"May I give you a goodnight kiss?"

Meredith answered by looking directly into his eyes.

He leaned forward and gently placed his lips on hers. The kiss was short, but he repeated it several times, each one a little longer. The last one was followed by the devastating smile. By then Meredith's abdomen was hosting a swarm of out-of-control locusts. Mark lay back down and closed his eyes.

"Goodnight, Mni-ha ha."

"'Night, Nagweyaab."

I want to be near him, yet this is a little unexpected and weird. I have just met him under extreme circumstances, and here he is inviting me to spend the night next to him. But recollections of the previous night convinced her that his invitation was innocent. She felt safe with him in every way. He knew everything about the wilderness. He could command bears. He was the most extraordinary person she had ever met. But the most extraordinary thing about him was the powerful effect his presence had on her body chemistry. Both pleasurable and frightening, the sensation was addictive.

"Keep watching. They'll show up," Mark assured her as he placed a bended arm over his eyes. "They may even howl again in the morning. Let's get a few hours sleep, and tomorrow we'll find your wolf buddy."

Meredith settled back on her side facing Mark, her head propped on one elbow. She loved the way darkness eased so imperceptibly into the Canadian wilderness. Once the sun dropped out of sight, a thin veil like gray chiffon formed on the eastern front and crept westward, advancing on the strong line of blood orange lying low across the western horizon until the light was muted, like a filmy scarf draped over a bedroom lamp. Muted but not extinguished. She could still discern the smooth features of Mark's face, his skin the color of a hickory nut tight across his cheekbones, the sharp angle of his jaw, the straight line of his eyebrows, the masculine delineation of his lips. His hair, black and glowing in the dimness, lay on his shoulders, one strand over his neck. She had never noticed such human beauty in a male. Despite his youth, his manly presence was transforming her. She knew it. She felt it. The tomboy veneer had cracked. Each of his smiles had pulled a strip of it away until now she lay beside him in the new and delicate skin of a woman.

Se sat up, swiveled back around, and focused her attention on the hill. The sun had sunk below the horizon, leaving the western sky with a ruby glow. A black vee of Canada geese flew across the red sky, racing against the fading light with urgent honking.

The silhouette of a wolf appeared on the distant hillock. The animal lifted his muzzle toward the heavens and began to howl. Others took their place around him and joined in the celebration of the oncoming night, their utterings entering one by one like voices in a fugue. They fell silent from time to time. Then one would initiate the calling, and again others would join in, not only those on the hill, but some from distant areas of the forest. Something inside her resonated with the wild chorus. *I bet Wolfie is one of them.* She closed her eyes in an effort to distinguish her wolf's howl from the others.

A night breeze picked up and Meredith shivered. She slid under the tarp, lay down beside Mark, and moved closer to his warmth. He stirred, slipped an arm under her neck, and cradled her head in the crook of his shoulder. She lay there listening to the primordial vocalizing of the wolves, a haunting call that echoed through the ancient forest and found its way into the nethermost regions of her young soul which, anxious at first, released itself and yielded to the sound, allowing itself to be transported to a time before the invention of time when all creatures were governed by the arc of the sun and the waxing and waning of the moon.

When the wild chorus ended and the wolf shapes had dissipated against the darkening sky, Meredith lay still on Mark's shoulder. It felt so natural, so right, as if destiny had brought her to him, and him to her, as if it were all meant to be. *I must get some sleep. Tomorrow will be filled with more amazing things.* She quieted her thoughts and cleared her mind until, at last, there was no sound other than the hypnotic distant murmur of mni-ha ha.

* * *

Meredith awoke sometime during the dimness of the Canadian summer night. Mark was on his side facing her, his breathing soft and regular. She could discern the angle of his jaw, the smoothness of his skin, the glossy black hair that seemed to reflect the starlight. She studied his features, her mind full of wonder at what was happening between them. Was he her special one that her mother had foretold, the one that would touch her heart and mind? She was well aware of the effect he had on her body, creating an awakening so powerful that it could distort her perception of reality.

She rolled onto her back, pulled the tarp up to her chin, and closed her eyes. She tried to remember everything her mother had said in that little talk. It was so long ago and seemed so unimportant at the time, so far into the future, nothing to be concerned about. All she could really remember was that she would someday find the right person, but that physical urges could lead her astray. *Time. That was what Mama had said. It takes a long time to know for sure. But in some cases couldn't it be sudden? Or at least short?*

The repetitive low-pitched *whoo-whoo-whoo* of a Great Gray Owl interrupted her meditation on the opposite sex and brought her back to the reality of where she was. A flood of anxiety engulfed her body and brain.

What am I doing here, sleeping with a stranger in the bush, looking for a wolf I have little chance of finding, while Mama and Bobby are worried sick over me? I am thinking only of myself, my possible love-interest, my pet wolf. Search and Rescue planes are no doubt flying all over Manitoba desperately looking for a foolish teenage girl. Mama has probably already had a nervous breakdown and Bobby hasn't had a wink of sleep. I'll tell Mark tomorrow that he must help me get back to Baldwin Lake. But how?

Chapter Eleven

Karen was on the dock before six a.m. The lake was calm. Strips of gold, pink, and green in the eastern sky sparkled back at her from the gently undulating water. In spite of her anxiety, she breathed deeply, absorbing the tranquil beauty of the morning into her troubled spirit, then lifted her eyes skyward, searching, as if she expected the Cessna and her daughter to appear in the magic of sunrise.

Bobby, Willie, and Paul came down from the lodge about six-thirty.

Precisely at seven the rescue plane, a DeHavilland Otter touched down. As soon as the Otter landed, an outdoorsman type with weather-worn skin and a physique in prime condition, deplaned, introduced himself as Brad Atkins, shook hands with everyone, and took charge. He unfolded a detailed map of Northeastern Manitoba and squatted to spread it out on the dock in front of Bobby.

"Mr. Marsten, show me exactly where you think she was headed."

"Call me Bobby."

Both men knelt beside the map. Bobby indicated the lake where he felt sure Meredith had landed. Brad stood up, refolded the map, and stuck it in a pocket of his jacket.

"Bobby, I understand that you, your wife, and Willie are riding with me in the search plane. I think we'd better get started."

Karen liked Brad's no-nonsense attitude. Within minutes they were ready to take off from Baldwin Lake to resume the search. Bobby was designated copilot, Karen and Willie were directed to sit in the passenger seats behind the cockpit, acting as lookouts, one at each window.

As they taxied out Bobby turned around to the lookouts.

"With four pairs of eyes searching, we'll have a better chance to spot the Cessna . . . or any kind of signal. Be sure to fasten your seatbelts back there."

As if we didn't know to do that, Bobby. Karen kept the retort silent. *He's just trying to be reassuring, to himself as well as to me.* She fastened the belt.

The pilot opened the throttle.

The plane skimmed along the surface of the water gaining momentum, lifted off, and reached altitude—high enough to be safe, low enough to see clearly below. Karen began looking immediately. *She could be anywhere. Maybe she didn't make it all the way to Wolfie's drop-off point. Maybe she didn't get very far at all.*

Karen had always loved flying over the wilderness. The vastness of it never ceased to amaze and excite her. Now it overwhelmed and frightened her. It had engulfed her daughter. Anxiety and desperation took hold of her throat, her chest, her stomach. She focused on every fraction of land and water beneath her, squinting to sharpen her vision. Several times she thought she saw something like the tail of a plane sticking out of a body of water then realized it was only a bolder, a small island, a rocky reef, or a group of fallen trees. After a long while, dizzy from the rapid eye movement and intense visual strain, she sat back and shut her eyes. When she opened them again, Bobby was pointing something out to the pilot. The Otter slowed, dropped down, and banked. They were landing.

Karen pressed her forehead against the window. All she could see was water. As the plane straightened out above the lake, she could see the thickly wooded shoreline. Then the Cessna came into view. *Maybe Meredith's inside. And safe, completely unharmed. But last night she was near the wolves. I could hear them. And she's not alone. I sensed that. Oh, God, what is happening to me? Am I losing my mind?*

Bobby and the pilot slid out of the cockpit into the water, turned the Otter around, and moored it next to the Cessna. The two planes sat side by side facing open water. With due caution Karen crawled from the back seat after the men were out. Willie helped her descend into the thigh-deep water. Bobby had already climbed into the other plane. He reappeared at the door.

"She's not here," he reported.

"Did she leave a note?" Karen struggled to hurry through the water, twisting from side to side.

"I don't see anything. But it looks like she has been sleeping here."

Taking her husband's hand, she came aboard and searched the plane for herself.

"She's probably out scavenging for food. Remember Emil said she made a couple of sandwiches and took some biscuits the morning she left. I'm sure that's all gone by now."

"Hey! There're footprints on the shore," Willie called. He was squatted, scrutinizing the ground. Bobby and Karen scrambled out of the Cessna and sloshed to shore.

"She definitely left the plane and walked along the shoreline for a while," Bobby concluded after examining the footprints.

"And there are ashes from a little fire on a rock over here," Brad said.

Karen mentally reconstructed her daughter's activities after landing. *She looked around for a place to build a signal fire. Then, for some reason, she decided to move along the shoreline and most likely entered the bush—alone.* "Was there any kind of weapon in the plane she could use?"

"Not that I know of. And probably no flares. Paul was about to fly it back to Winnipeg for the winter, have it serviced and re-equipped." Bobby shook his head.

"So she's out there defenseless. Oh, my God!"

"Karen, she has been taught to survive in the wild. And she'll do it. Brad, Willie and I will go looking for her. You stay here with the planes in case she comes back. I did bring a rifle with me and the pilot has one. There's a cooler full of food and drink in the Otter."

Bobby waded back to the rescue plane and returned to shore with a rifle over one shoulder and a canteen over the other. He had put on his heavy jacket.

"I've got snacks, water, and ammunition. I promise you, we will find her. We won't be long. She knows better than to wander away from the plane. She can't be very far."

"If she were nearby, wouldn't she have heard the Otter landing?"

"She may well have and is on her way as we speak. That's why you need to stay here." He turned toward the others. "Okay, guys, let's go find her." Now Bobby had taken command. Three men, two rifles, and a canteen disappeared into the bush. Karen remained in the cove. Karen and two unmanned floatplanes.

* * *

Worry and guilt weighed on Paul's spirit.

Dear God, please let them find her—unharmed. I know it's my fault. I should never have left the plane. I should have told Bobby the situation and asked him to go to Connor for help. Forgive me for thinking I could do it myself. The girl is innocent. She's just a young girl who has learned to fly. Nobody can blame her. It's all my fault. Please don't let the girl endure any hardship because of my mistakes.

Meredith had been missing for over twenty-four hours. With every passing minute Paul's misery worsened. With every tick of the wall clock in the lodge office, his chest tightened. Find her or not, he felt sure he would lose his job, maybe even his license.

After all these years of flying for Bobby. How could I have done such a thing? Maybe I'm getting old and can't think straight anymore. Maybe I should just quit flying. I don't want to endanger any lives—any other lives. Connor might hire me for something—take inventory or answer the phone, some no-risk position.

But Paul knew that first and foremost he was a bush pilot. He loved the job. He couldn't envision doing anything else. It was not *making a living*, it was *living*. When he was in the air above the wilderness he felt alive. He was close enough to the earth to admire the unique shape of each of the myriads of lakes that perforated the land, to spot a caribou or elk herd, to enjoy a flock of geese flying in formation below him. Yet he was high enough to see the ever-changing Canadian sky from pole to pole. It was the only life he had ever known, the only life he had ever wanted. So he prayed—about finding Meredith, about keeping his job, about Bobby's kind-heartedness and forgiveness.

At least he was helping out by staying behind to run the lodge for Bobby. The four hunters had settled their bar bills with him and were happily headed back to Winnipeg on Big Bear with photos of their own big bear they managed to down in the last hours of the hunt. The camp was still. Emil was quietly preparing a small dinner for the two guides and himself. Paul wasn't hungry.

His eyes were stinging from the constant clock-watching and from double- and triple- checking the figures on the bar bills. He drew a handkerchief from a back pocket and wiped them. When he stuffed the handkerchief into a jacket pocket, he felt the wetness and realized it was not the strain that was causing his eyes to sting and tear up, he was crying.

The tears and repentance brought some relief from the guilt that was causing him so much agony. Fresh air. That's what he needed. He pushed himself away from the desk, walked through the dining room to the sliding glass door, stepped out onto the deck, and took a deep breath of clean forest air. It filled him with determination to make all the wrongs right. After all, he was a good pilot, he had helped rescue a number of people stranded in the wilderness. He could land safely on lakes that required special skills. He always exercised good judgment. He had never even had a close call or done the least bit of damage to a plane. He didn't make mistakes—until now.

It's just my time to make one, I guess. Oh, God, please let this turn out okay for all of us. I will do anything—go to church on Sundays, give money to charity, visit people in prison, whatever you want . . . just, right now, let them find a clue to her whereabouts.

* * *

The men struggled with the underbrush, tearing, pushing and pulling at bushes and vines, Willie behind Bobby, with Brad acting as rear guard. They crept along, looking for any kind of path.

"We should have brought Tom with us. He's an expert at tracking."

"You're pretty good at it yourself, Bobby," Willie said.

"Not good enough." He ducked under a group of low branches and found what looked to him like a bear path—fit for four-legged beast but not for upright animals, yet better than no path at all.

"Watch for any trace of clothing, hair, broken twigs at waist-to-shoulder height." Bobby inspected every tree trunk, every bush, every inch of ground he passed. Every few paces he would shout her name: "Me-re-dith! Where are you? It's me, Bobby."

They stepped into an open area where the underbrush thinned out and the men could stand up straight. The trail seemed to end there. The thickness of the surrounding brush created an impasse.

"Over here, Bobby." Brad was down on one knee examining the base of a white pine. "Looks like something was here. The grass is flattened and scuffed."

Bobby dropped down on both knees beside the pilot. "You're right. And look." He pulled a long, brown curly hair from the tree bark. "It's hers. Thank God. We're on her trail. Keep your eyes sharp."

Willie made a full 380-degree turn. "Which way from here, Bobby? The path sorta ends. Maybe she got this far, rested for a while, then went back to the plane."

"I don't think so. I saw quite a few branches bent forward but none bent back the other way," Brad said.

"I noticed that, too." Bobby lifted his cap, ran his fingers through his dark curls, then reset the cap. "Okay, guys. Let's see if we can find another path. It may be pretty low to the ground if it's used primarily by smaller animals, like martens and rabbits. One of us will find something that tells us which direction she took." He went back to scrutinizing tree trunks, limbs, branches, and twigs. "Check every square centimeter."

The three men worked in silence for a few minutes, checking bushes and tree trunks, and scouring the ground for any clue.

"This forest sure hides evidence. No footprints in the thick floor. No trace of anything. I haven't even seen any animal scat." Willie stood up and stretched his back.

"Come on, Willie. Don't start thinking like that," Bobby warned. "We've got to be positive . . . and alert." He switched his rifle to the other shoulder and pushed pass a large shrub.

"Hey, I've found something else," he called to the others. "A partial footprint."

Brad and Willie joined him. Bobby pointed to a small patch of soft earth.

"Lug sole. It's got to be hers."

Willie took off his cap and scratched his bald pate. "Guess I have to eat my words."

"Looks like this is the path. You sure couldn't tell from the other side of that chokecherry bush. Good work, Bobby." Brad gave him a gentle slap on the shoulder. "Let's move on. And Bobby, keep calling her."

With hope and strength renewed by the hair and the footprint, Bobby pressed on, followed by his two companions in the search, each of them taking turns calling out to Meredith. After a while they fell silent. Bobby knew the men were tired and thirsty.

"Let's take a short break." He unscrewed the cap of the canteen, took a sip of water, and handed it to Brad who then passed it to Willie.

He took a long swallow and wiped his mouth on his sleeve. "How are we going to find our way back?"

"I've been marking trees with a slash ever since we left the shore. I can get us back," Bobby reassured him. He reached into a pocket then opened his fist to reveal a pocket knife, blade folded in. "I always keep this sharp and handy."

"I should have known you'd think of everything." He handed the water back to Bobby. "How long are we going to keep looking?"

"Until we find her," he said and tightened the cap back on the canteen.

* * *

Bobby, a good distance ahead of the other men, was the first to come to the camp. Before calling out, he stood still, keeping himself concealed and listening for any sound of life in or around the wigwam. A strong odor of smoke and a faint aroma of cooked meat. There had been a campfire recently and someone had eaten. He stepped out and walked around to the front of the wigwam.

"Hello. Anyone here? Boozhoo. Gidab ina?"

No response. Bobby pulled open the flap and ducked inside. A large bearskin pallet took up most of the space. A lantern and a stack of books set next to the bed. There were a few tin dishes, some clothing, several boxes of rifle shells, a folding chair, and matches. No Meredith.

"Bobby? Are you here?" Brad and Willie had arrived in the campsite. Bobby came out of the wigwam and closed the flap.

"Anything in there?" Willie asked.

"Just the bare essentials for surviving life in the bush."

"Obviously an Indian camp," Brad said.

"Yes, a lot like Tom has over at Poplar River. Let's take a good look around. I believe she's been here."

"I think you're right. Here're some more of those lug sole prints." Willie pointed to an area beside the fire ring.

"Okay, then. She probably ate the sandwiches and spent the first night in the plane. Then yesterday she got hungry and went looking for food. She may have smelled the meat cooking. Spent the night here," Bobby calculated.

Willie raised an eyebrow. "With whoever lives here? Could that person have taken her captive and forced her to come here?"

"First Nations people offer hospitality, Willie. They trap animals, not people."

Brad interrupted. "I bet they've gone fishing. Seems logical, if she's hungry."

"That's a good thought, Brad. Perhaps we should be out on the lake looking for a canoe." Bobby said.

"Speaking of hungry, we haven't eaten all day."

"I'm aware of that fact, Willie."

Bobby fished three Snickers bars out of a jacket pocket. "Here. Take one of these. Willie and Brad each helped themselves. Bobby put the other one back.

The men sat on the ground to eat. Bobby passed the canteen again.

He knew the others were worn out from battling the bush. So was he. Brad leaned back against a spruce and closed his eyes. Willie stretched out to catch a quick nap. Bobby walked around the camp then sat on a large cylinder of a cut tree trunk by the fire pit. He propped an elbow on his thigh and rested his chin in the cup of his hand, trying to decide what to do next. Logic told him that Meredith had not returned to the plane but rather left the camp with the aboriginal, no doubt to look for the wolf. Finally he stood.

"It's getting late. We'd better head back to the Otter. Meredith could be there with Karen by now. If not, we'll come here tomorrow to pick up her trail. Just follow my slash marks." He pointed to a slanted gouge mark about shoulder level in the trunk of a poplar. "I estimate we're about three hours away if we move fast and don't get lost."

Light was beginning to fade, and there were distant rumblings of thunder.

"Should one of you stay here . . . in case she and . . . the native come back to the camp tonight?" Brad asked.

"We'll leave a note for her, telling her to follow my marked trail back to the floatplane tomorrow morning and wait for us there."

After some searching, they located pencil and paper among the books in the primitive dwelling. Bobby wrote the message and attached it to the flap of the wigwam with a fish hook from a pack in the wigwam.

Muffin: If you find this tonight, in the morning follow the slash marks that begin on the trees to your left as you exit the wigwam. Keep them on your left and they will take you to the floatplane. Your mother and I will pick you up there. We are praying you are okay. We love you.
Bobby

Before leaving the camp, Bobby took out his pocket knife and made more slash marks in the trees to the left of the wigwam.

* * *

Karen's jeans were wet up to the thigh, and the wind coming off the lake was chilly. But waiting in either plane was not an option—they both faced the lake. She needed a clear view of the shoreline to see her daughter if and when she emerged from the bush. Taking a knit cap out of a jacket pocket, she pulled it low over her ears. She found a boulder to sit on, turned her back to the wind, and waited.

Please come back, Sugar Baby. I'm here, waiting for you. Oh, God, please let them find her. I'll do anything you want me to, I promise, just don't take her away from me.

She continued to alternate between pleas, prayers, and promises until the discomfort of her rock-hard seat became too much. She slid down the rock and sat cross-legged on the ground. When her folded legs began to ache, she stretched them out. The sun was higher and warmer now. Her jeans were drying out. She leaned back against the boulder and closed her eyes.

. . ."*Mama! Mama! I found Wolfie!*" *Meredith appeared at the edge of the woods holding a starving wolf pup. Then Bobby was there beside her. "We have to take him back." He lifted the pup from her arms, turned, and walked back into the forest. Meredith began to sob. "It'll be okay, Sugar Baby." Karen tried to go to comfort her daughter but her legs and arms were so heavy she couldn't move them . . . .*

A blowing sound startled Karen from her dream. In a nano-second her eyes were wide open. She dared not breathe. There at the water's edge, not ten feet away, was a large, muscular creature, his head raised, water dripping from a tremendous rack. He stood in profile to her.

The moose blew again, clearing his nose of any remaining water, but he did not move. A feral eye rolled back to have a look at the other creature sharing the beach with him. His eye met hers only for a fleeting moment, but in that brief meeting so much passed between them: *I am not afraid of you, but I do live with fear, fear that makes me cautious at all times. And caution is one of the instincts that guide my existence. Unlike me, you are guided by reason, a guide much less secure than mine.*

Taking his time, the moose turned away from the water, away from Karen, and ambled without a sound into the forest. The only noise Karen could hear was that of her own heart pounding in her ears. Finally she was calm enough to stand up, and as she did, a strange feeling came over her, a sense of tragedy so strong that she almost fell. She covered her face with her hands and opened her mind. Then she understood. She knew. The moose was heading to his death.

* * *

In the late afternoon Karen retreated to the Cessna. The interior would be warm from the sun. She had paced up and down the shore calling her daughter—to no avail. She was tired and hungry, and there was food in the Otter, but she chose to wait in the Cessna where there were traces of Meredith. Biscuit crumbs, a blanket bed, the map, and the log book that recounted the storm and the forced landing. She tried to envision what Meredith endured, fighting the elements to land without power, without a radio, and without an emergency locater. How could this have happened? They were always so careful. And why was she so sure that the moose was going to die? She felt that normal life had been put on hold and that she was in some kind of time warp or reality distortion. Where was Bobby? Why had they been gone so long? Her head was full of questions. Her heart was full of pain.

You have another child to think about now.

Of course Bobby was right. But that child was safe in her womb, warm and fed, while Meredith was somewhere out there under who-knows-what circumstances, lost, hungry, exhausted, frightened, alone—well, maybe not alone.

If only there was something I could do. This waiting, not knowing anything, is unbearable.

Raucous screams of crows attracted her attention. She leaned toward a rear window and looked at the sky. Two black birds were harassing a bald eagle, taking turns rushing at him in swooping dives. The eagle flew first one way and then the other to avoid their attacks. His squealing sounds seemed so innocent compared to the raspy cries of the crows.

How could so powerful a bird as an eagle be intimidated by two silly crows? He must have flown too close to their nesting area. Do crows nest this late in the season?

Leaning forward with her nose pressed against the window of the Cessna Karen relived her first encounter with the wilderness and its creatures. The honeymoon. She remembered her apprehension when Steve helped her climb up into the little floatplane. She had sat where she was seated now. She remembered staring in amazement at the scene beneath the plane as she flew over the wilderness for the first time—seventeen years ago. She had forgotten many of the details of that flight, but the memory of a bald eagle flying alongside the plane as it descended into Poplar River outpost was still vivid. Nor could she ever forget that moment when the eagle's eye focused directly on her. Like the moose's eye today.

When the aerial dispute ended with the eagle's retreat, the marauding crows disappeared into the tree tops. Karen shook memories from her head and returned to present concerns. Because she could not see much of the shoreline from the plane, she considered climbing back out. But the idea of dipping her legs and dry jeans back into the water made her think better of it. She would depend on her ears to alert her to any arrival, human or otherwise. The red glow of the setting sun filtered in through the cockpit windows.

It's getting late. They'll have to come back soon if we are to fly home tonight. Lord, please let Meredith be with them, please!

Within minutes Karen heard voices.

"She must be in one of the planes." Willie's voice.

"Karen!" Bobby called.

She moved to the pilot's seat, opened the door, and leaned out.

"I'm here," she waved to the men.

Three men, with two rifles and a canteen, came out of the bush. Meredith was not with them.

Karen slid down the struts, squatted on the float, and slipped into the water. Bobby, Paul, and Willie stood on shore passing the canteen.

"You didn't find her?"

"We were hoping she had come back here," Bobby said. He went to meet Karen as she came out of the water and put his arm around her shoulder.

"We did find evidence," he said.

"What kind of evidence?"

"We found an aboriginal campsite where she must have spent the second night. We saw imprints of her boots and found a strand of hair that has to be hers. She's with someone."

"Who? Where are they?" Karen was grasping at straws.

"That's all we know, Sweetheart."

"Why is she not there now?"

"They may have gone fishing or hunting for food."

"But it's getting late."

"There's still a couple hours of daylight. And we need to take off for home while it's still safe to fly."

Bobby turned to the men who were sitting on the beach devouring sandwiches the pilot had fetched from the Otter.

"Okay, guys. Let's get airborne. We'll pick up her trail at first light."

"No, Honey. I'm not going back. I'm staying here. I'll sleep in the Cessna the way she did. She may come back by dark."

"Not a good idea, Karen." Bobby shook his head. "She's not going to wander the woods at night. She knows better. And so do you. There's no point to it, and besides, it could be dangerous."

"What do you mean?"

"A storm could come up and we couldn't get back tomorrow. You'd be stranded."

Karen thought it over. She still would prefer to stay—just in case—but Bobby seemed to be the voice of reason. In thinking of her well-being, she knew he was also thinking of his own child. She did need to eat, bathe, get some rest, and take her vitamins.

"All right, I'll go with you. But I don't think I can endure another night knowing that she is in the wilderness so far from us. With some person, a stranger."

Ominous clouds so deep a gray that they appeared blue rolled in like malevolent spirits seeking to spread doom. A distant chorus of wolves began to howl, adding a portentous sound to the sky's menace.

The more she thought about it, the more disturbed she became. Overcome by a feeling of helplessness, she fell silent and obediently settled in the back seat of the Otter.

What if the weather really does keep us from getting back up here tomorrow? If Meredith sleeps at the Indian camp again tonight will she stay warm and dry? Does she have a change of underwear? Of clothes? Karen had to fight hard to keep from telling the pilot to cut the engine and let her out.

During the flight home she occupied herself with memories of times shared with her daughter. Her first birthday party and the gigantic panda bear her father had given her, the squeal of delight she always emitted when Karen modeled a gown chosen for an orchestral appearance or recital, her daughter's futile attempts to submit to piano lessons from her mother, the first fish she caught—a small walleye that she removed from the hook by herself and released back into the water, her romps with Wolfie, her laughter, her energy, her beauty—both outer and inner. With myriad images swirling in her head, Karen slept until the floats touched down on Baldwin Lake.

* * *

At bedtime Karen's prayers were long and fervent and continued well after she had slipped under the covers. She turned on her side to face her husband.

"Promise me we won't come back to the lodge until we find her. I don't care if it takes weeks."

"I agree. We'll take sleeping bags and plenty of food and supplies this time. I think Willie is going back to Winnipeg—he has to get back to his job at Connor, but Paul will be with us. Cedric and Tom are back in camp now. The last of the hunters settled their accounts and flew out on Big Bear." He reached over and stroked her hair. "We're not coming back without her."

Bobby's words were soothing to her anxious mind. She nestled closer and put her head on his shoulder. *How lucky I am to have Bobby. If anyone can find her, he can.*

Her eyes blinked open before daybreak. Anxiety flooded back into her brain, her chest, and her abdomen. She turned to wake up Bobby, but his side of the bed was empty. She threw back the covers, slipped on a robe, and hurried toward the lodge kitchen. When she passed Meredith's storage closet-bedroom, she stopped. She opened the door, switched on the light and stood looking at her daughter's personal space. The girl's fresh woodsy fragrance, still lingered. The single bed was made and everything seemed in place. The wall peg that usually held her jacket was empty.

Drawn by a desire to immerse herself in Meredith's aura, she stepped inside and closed her eyes. Taking deep breaths she spoke aloud, believing that mother and child could communicate beyond physical limitations.

"My Baby Girl, I miss you so much. I'm sure you know that we are looking for you as hard as we can. Don't take any chances. Remember everything Bobby has taught you about survival in the wilderness. And wait for us. We are coming to get you today. You are so precious to me. I love you with all my heart."

Wiping her eyes on the sleeve of her robe. She closed the door, hurried through the staff dining room and pushed open the door to the lodge kitchen. She found Bobby and Emil bent over a large cooler, filling it with food packages wrapped in aluminum foil.

"We'll be ready to take off in about twenty minutes, Honey. Better get dressed. Oh, and don't forget to take a change of underwear," Bobby closed the cooler and grinned at her.

"There are some blueberry muffins I made on the counter next to ze coffee pot. Eat somesing before you go, Madame." Emil was wearing his toque even at this hour.

It seems like everybody is telling me what to do this morning.

Karen reached into a pocket of her robe and took out a bottle of prenatal vitamins, walked over to the muffins and coffee, and ate a fast breakfast standing at the counter. She took a vitamin with the last bite of muffin. Twenty minutes later she was fastening her seat belt and looking out at the brilliant gold and purple hues of the eastern sky that signaled the rising of the sun, like the hope rising in her heart.

Chapter Twelve

"Wake up, Mni-ha ha. It's wolf day."

Meredith stretched her arms out from under the warm tarpaulin and took a deep breath of the forest air. The smell of spruce and pine mingled with the lingering smoky aroma of last night's fire. She sat up. She knew it was early, for the eastern sky was crimson and the birds had not yet begun their morning hopping and chirping.

"I'm going to check some of my traps. Grilled rabbit would make a nice breakfast. I'll leave the rifle here. You know how to use one?"

"If I have to." She yawned. *I guess I can.* She had no clue.

"You can rebuild the fire while I'm gone. It'll save time. I'll only be a few minutes. Or you can come with me if you prefer."

"It's pretty chilly. I think I'll build a fire and get warm." *That I can do.*

Mark reached into his jacket pocket.

"Here're some matches. Fire the rifle if you need me." He tossed the pack of matches onto the tarp.

Meredith nodded and gave him a smile. *I think I will always need you.*

* * *

True to his word, Mark returned shortly holding a rather large rabbit.

"Fire looks good," he said.

"It feels even better." She eyed the creature in Mark's hand. "I can build fires, but I don't skin rabbits."

"I'll take care of that. Find us some long, thin green branches to use as skewers."

Mark pulled his knife from its sheath and laid the rabbit on a large rock.

"Poor bunny," Meredith said and turned away from the primitive operation.

"I bet you'll eat 'poor bunny.'" Mark set to the task.

Meredith found the sticks. Marked stripped them, sharpened them, and slid three choice chunks of meat on the ends of each. "Hope you like shish kebabs. I seasoned them with some herbs I picked on the way back."

They sat roasting their meaty breakfast in the flames. Meredith blew on an end chunk, slipped it off the skewer, and popped it into her mouth.

"It's really good." She took another bite. "Is there anything you can't do?"

"I can't fly a plane." He wiped his mouth on the back of his hand and smiled. Meredith's insides fluttered to the point of pain. But she had no trouble finishing her rabbit kabob.

"There's more meat," Mark offered.

"Gosh, no thanks. People won't believe I've spent days in the bush if I come back fat."

"Well, then it's time to find your wolf. We'll walk over to the rendez-vous area, and you can call him. I bet he'll come to you . . . if he's alive."

They made sure the fire was stamped out and the tarp folded and hung back in its place. Mark sheathed his knife, picked up the rifle, and led the way.

They came to a small clearing within sight of the howling mound. Mark stopped.

"The wolves are usually in the bush on the other side of the clearing. Especially in the morning. Other times they roam around a pretty wide area. Go ahead. Call your wolf."

Meredith walked to the center of the clearing. With her hands cupped around her mouth she called:

"Wo-ol—fie. Here boy! Come, Wo-olfie!" She repeated the call several times.

Each time they waited in silence, turning to look and listen in all directions.

Meredith's shoulders slumped in a hopeless sigh. "I guess he's forgotten . . . or maybe he's . . . ." She couldn't bear to say the word *dead*.

A movement in the bushes caught her attention. She stood still as a boulder. A tiny wolf head emerged through the branches. Then another. She looked back at Mark and pointed, mouthing the words "wolf pups." She sat down. The curious pups poked their heads in and out of the bushes until their curiosity got the best of them, and they came forth. In a series of three-steps-forward-then-two-steps-back motions they approached Meredith. Just as she reached out to touch one, a fully-grown wolf charged out of the woods, stopping short of Meredith and the pups. Meredith jumped to her feet and ran toward Mark. Rather than give chase to the intruder, the wolf went to the pups. They crouched behind the adult protector. Within seconds four or five more grown wolves appeared in the clearing, some went to the pups, others stood snarling, fangs bared.

"What do we do, Mark?" she asked in a desperate whisper.

"Stay calm and back away slowly. They're protecting the pups. They don't want us."

Meredith took a few shaky steps back. The wolves didn't move. All of a sudden the largest one bounded toward her. Mark drew his knife and rushed toward the attacking animal.

"No, Mark, no!" she screamed. "I think it's Wolfie!"

The wolf slowed and stopped in front of her. She held a trembling hand out to him. He lowered his head, took a few cautious steps toward the fingers, stretched his heavily-furred neck forward, and sniffed.

"Wolfie," Meredith whispered. "It's me." At the sound of her voice the thick tail began to wag, slightly at first, then harder and harder until his whole body was twisting. Meredith went down on one knee. Wolfie raised his muzzle and started licking her face. Her arms went around her beloved wolf's neck. Tears rolled onto his fur. Extreme fear became supreme joy.

"Oh, Wolfie," she cried. "I've missed you so much. You're so big now."

She stood up, keeping a hand on Wolfie's head.

"Mark, it *is* him. Isn't he beautiful?"

Mark shook his head in amazement. "I almost killed him. You certainly are brave."

Wolfie started away, turned and came back to her, started away again, and returned.

"He wants me to go with him."

Meredith followed. Wolfie led her straight to the pups. She knelt in front of them and petted their ears and necks. The adult that had appeared first seemed to be the mother of the two young wolves. She licked the foreheads and ears of the pups. Wolfie touched his nose to hers. Mark walked over to Meredith and knelt beside her.

"I think she's Wolfie's mate, but the pups are too old to be his."

"He must have adopted a family," Meredith concluded.

"Looks like he's the leader of the pack."

"I always knew he would be."

"He's a fine specimen of a wolf. I glad I didn't have to kill him."

"But Mark, you were so brave."

"Isn't that what I just said about you?"

Meredith gave a half smile. *How close the two of us have grown in such a short time. I feel as though he is my best friend, even closer than Wolfie now.*

One by one the other wolves disappeared into the forest, leaving Meredith and Mark with their leader, his mate, and her pups. Meredith spent a little more time with her wolf and his family. *He's so much more beautiful than the others. He's bigger, his coat is luxurious. He's endowed with leadership qualities. And he's providing for some orphan pups—just the way we provided for him. And the female seems like a good mother. Next season he will probably have pups of his own, and Mark and I will come back to see them.*

Satisfied that Wolfie had adapted in remarkable fashion to the wilderness, Meredith turned to her human companion:

"They make a fine couple, don't you think?"

Mark gazed at her. "A great couple."

Something about that answer sent a hot flash through her chest. She regained her composure and stood watching her wolf and his forest family. She looked back at Mark.

"I think we can go home now. I know that Wolfie has a good life, that he's okay and that he has not forgotten me. Thank you so much for bringing me here. I will always, always appreciate your kindness." She wiped tears of joy from her cheeks.

Mark stood and put an arm around her shoulders. "Come, Mni-ha ha, I'll take you back to my camp, and we will find a way to get you home."

Meredith turned to leave Wolfie, but the wolf ran to her side.

"Looks like your wolf wants to keep you company," Mark said.

"I don't think he intends to go back home with me. He's got some big responsibilities here. Maybe he just wants to escort us out of his territory."

"Let him come along."

"We really don't have a choice, do we?"

They found the trail again and started the journey home. The sound of the waterfall grew louder as they passed nearby.

"Another shower?" Mark teased.

"No, but I'll be happy to turn my back, if you want to take one."

"I think we'd better move along if we want to reach the camp before dark."

The wind picked up. Darker clouds blew in from the north. Meredith and Mark walked in silence for a while, the only sound that of the wolf's panting at Meredith's heels.

"We've been really lucky with our weather. We could have had thunderstorms. They're prevalent around here," Mark said.

"Don't speak too soon," Meredith warned, half serious. "Have you noticed the sky?"

"Yeah. It could start raining before we make it back. Then I guess we'll both get a shower."

"I'd prefer mni-ha ha."

Wolfie suddenly ran ahead.

"Now where's he going?" Mark asked.

"Maybe he's scouting the route for us. He used to do that for me on the lodge grounds."

"Will we get to swing over the ravine again?" Meredith asked.

"As many times as you like."

"It made me feel like Tarzan."

"You mean like Jane."

"No, like Tarzan," she said with a sassy upward tilt of her chin.

* * *

Mark slowed his pace to allow the girl to lead the way. This young woman was so different from all other girls he had known. Ebullience showed in her movements, joy in her laugh, radiance in her smile. She was natural. She loved the wilderness. She was open to new ideas, new adventures. There was something wild in her nature, yet she was down-to-earth, often revealing a pragmatic side. She was smart—she had to be to learn how to fly a plane at her age. Or maybe his fascination with her was mainly because of her curly hair and her eyes, both the color of a snowshoe rabbit in summer. So many things about her amused him—the way she could tease him, the way she would understand and laugh at his subtle humor, the way she turned her head to one side like a bird when she was listening. Her curiosity pleased him—she asked questions about his people and their customs. She wanted to know more about the forest and its creatures. She showed no fear. From what he could tell, she was a tomboy who had blossomed into a beautiful woman. The combination of femininity and boyish spirit of adventure charmed him beyond words.

And she aroused him. He had slept beside her under the tarp and felt her warmth like that of a mother fox. Her breathing as she slept reminded him of water rippling in the night wind. He wanted to keep her with him, hold her in his arms every night, and teach her all the secrets of nature he had learned from Nokomis. The kiss they had shared last night still burned in his blood. She had come to him the way Nokomis said she would. She came to him in the wilderness, alone—as if she had come to find *him*. Perhaps she had.

"One day you will find love, or rather love will find you when and where you least expect it. Her smile will hover in your mind like mist on the river. You will hear her voice in the shiver of poplar leaves in the wind. Wait for her, my son, alone in the forest she will come to you. You will love her and no other."

He had never forgotten his grandmother's last words to him. He stood beside her bed and held her worn hand. She was the most special person in the world to him. She had told him ancestral stories and taught him the ways of the wilderness. In her late years wisdom gave her insight into the future. He always listened to her. He always believed her. So did they all, the whole family. Grandfather revered her and moved in orbit around her sunny radiance. She was the matriarch.

"Hey, come on! Are you daydreaming?" Meredith turned around to Mark whose musings had made him fall behind.

"Just watching to see if you can stay on the path and not get lost like you did the other day."

"Not fair."

"Actually I was admiring your shapely figure and your sprightly step." Mark decided to tell the truth.

"Well . . . , make *your* step a little more sprightly. Wolfie's getting way ahead."

"Yes, *Minnie*."

He caught up with his companion, took her by the arm and turned her toward him.

"I really meant it. You are beautiful, and smart . . . and a little wild."

He cupped her head between his hands, lacing her brown curls between his fingers, and gently turned her face to him.

"This will not be a little 'good night' kiss," he whispered.

He brought his lips to hers and kissed her, gently at first, then, giving in to desire, he drew her body tight against him and pressed his mouth harder against hers. When his tongue slid into her mouth, she wrapped her arms around his chest. Through both of their jackets he could feel the firm mounds of her breasts and the pounding of her heart against his own. He withdrew his lips and, with his cheek alongside hers, said to her what he had never said to anyone before.

"Gi zah gin, Mnihaha."

"I love you, too, Mark."

Releasing the embrace, Mark looked into her eyes. Flecks of gold created by the dappled sunlight shone like fire in her pupils.

"How did you know what I said?"

"I . . . I'm not sure. I just knew."

She is so much like Nokomis. Sensitive, wise, and full of love and laughter.

"What am I going to do with you?" Mark shook his head. "I want you to stay with me, not only here in the forest, but everywhere . . . and always. But you are so young. You have to finish high school, go to college, chose a career . . . ."

"And you have to finish your degree and start your career."

"That will be done by next summer."

Wolfie rejoined them and began circling the couple, vying for attention.

"Come, my bright little waterfall, we must get you back home or your parents will hate me."

"Oh, I don't think so. They'll be glad I finally have a romantic interest." She smiled, brought two fingers to her mouth, kissed them then placed them on Mark's lips. She brushed aside a low branch of a jack pine and stepped back on the path of their homeward journey.

Nokomis, you were right. She has come to me alone in the forest. Now I know how Mishomis felt about you. And, yes, I will love her and no other.

* * *

Meredith's joy was unbridled. She had found Wolfie. He was not only in good physical condition, but it also looked like he was faring well among the wolves. He had obviously adopted a mate and her pups. The entire pack seemed to be in obeisance to him. He *was* an alpha wolf, yet he remembered her. He was with her now—for a while, and so was Mark. That was the strange part. Her relationship with Mark had taken precedent over her relationship with Wolfie. Her devotion to the wolf was waning while the intensity of her feelings for her wilderness companion was waxing stronger.

How could you possibly be enamored of a guy you've just met? Could two days in the wilderness together inspire such a powerful emotion? Maybe I'm too young, too naïve. Is the first attraction always so powerful?

Meredith's heart was alternating rapidly between the old and the new—her old affection for Wolfie and her new-found passion for Mark. He was so handsome, so wise, so overwhelming to her sensibilities. She had trouble concentrating around him. She became acutely aware of all her flaws—her freckles, care-free hair and laissez-faire fingernails, her lack of knowledge about make-up. She had never considered herself sexy. But for the first time she was aware of her femininity despite the tomboy vestiges.

He seems to like me the way I am. Or maybe he's just amused by my awkwardness, or my teasing. All I know is I want his arms around me, his lips against mine. I want him to want me—in every way.

Meredith's thoughts had distracted her from Wolfie's presence. She felt guilty about that.

I'm here for my wolf, not for anything else, she counseled herself.

Mark had fallen behind. She called to him.

"Hey, come on. Are you daydreaming?"

"Just watching to see if you can stay on the path and not get lost like you did the other day."

"Not fair."

"Actually I was admiring your shapely figure and your sprightly step."

"Well . . . , make *your* step a little more sprightly. Wolfie's getting way ahead."

"Yes, *Minnie.*"

Meredith would relive the next few moments many times in next few months.

She felt Mark's hand on her forearm, turning her around toward him.

"This will not be a little 'goodnight' kiss." He pulled her close and pressed his lips against hers.

For the next few minutes she was totally engulfed in the man's presence, in his masculinity. His kiss became more passionate. She yielded her body to his as they stood embracing in the midst of the boreal forest. Her arms went around him as instinctively she pressed her body against his. When his tongue explored the inside of her mouth, she recognized it as the prelude of a more forceful urge to penetrate—and be penetrated, to become one.

I can't help it. I have fallen in love with this man.

Pinwheels were spinning fast in her brain and in her body. She became oblivious to everything around her. She was in a private universe that consisted only of the two of them. Mark pulled away and looked into her eyes. His gaze struck her heart with the force of an arrow.

I think I know what he is going to say.

He spoke some Ojibwe words she had never heard, but knew what they meant.

"Gi zah gin, Mni-ha-ha."

"I love you, too, Mark."

She had spoken from the heart. Nothing mattered now except being with Mark. She could not think about anything else. She wanted this moment to last forever. She wanted to stay in his arms forever, with the wind in the poplars repeating their whispered declarations of love *ad infinitum.*

When Mark began to talk of her future educational commitments, Meredith was propelled back into the reality of her situation. The momentary abandonment to romantic passion was checked.

"Come, my bright little waterfall, we must get you back home or your parents will hate me."

"Oh, I don't think so. They'll be glad I finally have a romantic interest." Meredith knew that her mother was concerned that she was not becoming a "proper young lady," southern style, with a respectable beau courting her. They recently had another mother-daughter discussion of the subject during a pre-bedtime snack of cocoa and crackers in the lodge kitchen.

"Sugar, aren't there some boys in your class at school?"

"Of course, Mama, there're plenty of them."

"Aren't any of them your friends?"

"They all are, except maybe one or two jerks." She bit off half a cracker and took a sip of the hot chocolate.

"I mean, isn't there one that's kind of special to you?"

"No, Mama, I don't have a boyfriend, if that's what you're getting at. If you met them you'd understand why not. They're all so boring. I doubt that I'll ever find anyone who interests me."

"I just want to be sure you're happy. I don't want the summers here at the lodge to keep you from enjoying your friends."

Meredith could hear the frustration in her mother's voice and watched as she turned her cup around and around in the saucer.

"Please don't fret over my lack of a love life. Most parents are worried about just the opposite. A lot of girls my age change boyfriends almost as often as they change clothes."

"You've got a point there. I'd be going crazy if you were running around and going out with different boys all the time." She looked long and hard at Meredith and seemed to come up with an idea.

"Would you like to spend next summer in Spring Hill with Granny and Papa Kinsley? You'd make friends and might meet a nice southern boy."

Meredith tightened her lips and let out an audible sigh.

"Like you did, Mama?"

Meredith took her cup to the sink, rinsed it, and placed it in the dishwasher. "I'm going to bed now." She gave her mother a kiss on the cheek and walked away.

I won that round.

She mentally reviewed family history on her way back to her closet room. After a brief courtship, her mother had married Steve Marsten, a professor of English at Heyward College in her home town of Spring Hill, South Carolina. Steve was born and raised in Iowa City with his cousin Bobby. Bobby's parents were killed in an automobile accident when he was a year old, and Steve's parents had raised the two boys together. A few years after Steve's suicide, Karen married Bobby. Her mother's two husbands were from the Midwest. So much for "a nice southern boy."

But Meredith knew her victory was pyrrhic. Her mother had experienced great love in both of her marriages. And with Bobby she found not only a romantic lead but also a soul mate.

That's what I want. I will not settle for less than what Mama has. I know Mark is the one. Or am I just young and inexperienced? After all, he's the first boy I've ever been attracted to, the first boy I've ever wanted.

* * *

Meredith tripped over some vines and almost lost her balance.

"Are you okay?" Mark leapt forward, ready to break her fall.

"I'm fine. Really. I just got distracted. I wonder why Wolfie has gone so far ahead?"

"Perhaps he's giving us some privacy."

Meredith couldn't help but smile. "You're probably right. He's a very sensitive wolf."

A little farther they found the moose carcass, partially eaten by ground and aerial scavengers. The sight was even more ungodly and the stench had worsened. Meredith held her breath as she walked past. She said nothing for a while, allowing the picture of the poor beast to fade from her mind.

They had come to the roughest part of the trail. Briars and branches, trees fallen against trees, late summer overgrowth of bushes and vines made the going difficult. Meredith had to watch every step.

"Hey, Mark. It looks like something has been dragged over the trail. See these lines . . . and those places where the moss has been scraped up?"

"I've noticed it ever since we left the moose. That's the poachers' bag with the moose head. One of the poachers must be hauling it. Probably to the the little beach where my boat is moored. That's where the last poachers were caught."

"Where were these guys last night?"

"Probably spent the night not too far from the kill. I worried that they may have gone to the wolf site for another trophy. Evidently they started back this morning."

"I wonder how they crossed the ravine?"

"They may not be there yet."

"You mean they're not far ahead of us?"

Her companion fell silent. Meredith sensed his apprehension.

Coming around a curve in the trail, Mark grabbed Meredith's arm and pulled her back. Wolfie was in a standoff with two men. One took his rifle from his shoulder, clicked a bullet into the chamber, and aimed at the wolf.

"Hold your fire," Mark yelled and rushed forward. Meredith didn't move a muscle.

"Who the hell are you?" the marksman asked, obviously stunned to encounter other humans.

"I live here. This is First Nations hunting ground. Show me your licenses to kill a wolf—and a moose. " Mark's voice was authoritative.

"First Nations hunting ground, huh?" I think it's *our* hunting grounds." He directed the barrel of his rifle toward Mark. He was tall and lanky with a couple of days' growth of scruffy beard. The other was shorter and stocky. Meredith thought he looked confused and uncomfortable with his partner's actions.

Wolfie let out a vicious growl and crouched to spring.

The marksman aimed again at Wolfie. "Fiend from hell!"

"Our wolf will attack if we command him to," Mark stated emphatically. "If you shoot him, I will shoot you." Mark raised his rifle.

"Look. We're hunters. We want no trouble," the shorter man said.

"What's in your bag? A moose head? I think that is illegal."

The poacher with the loaded gun spoke.

"It's none of your business. I think you two are our prisoners, now, as well as your wolf. We have two guns to your one. Keep quiet and no one will get hurt. Lower your weapon. Lay your weapon on the ground or I'll shoot either the girl or the wolf."

Mark complied. But Wolfie didn't. He kept growling and prepared to spring.

"Call off your wolf, or he'll make a nice, easy trophy," the tall guy said.

"Here, Wolfie, come," Meredith coaxed. The wolf obeyed his former mistress, came to her side, but stood growling.

"That's better. Now, we're going to walk back along the trail until we reach our canoe where my partner and I will wait for a plane that's coming to pick us up. Understood? Then the three of you werewolves can go along your merry way. Clear? All right, move out."

The taller thin guy was obviously the more dangerous of the two, and he had taken charge. He motioned for his companion to pick up the young man's rifle.

The group of four humans and one wolf set out southward bound along the trail, Mark leading the way, then Meredith and Wolfie, the man with the rifle behind them, and the short fellow at the rear of the procession, struggling with the large game bag and the guns.

This is one time that Mark is not in control. And neither is Wolfie. I wonder if these guys really plan to let us go. That would be dumb of them, since we can identify them and put an end to their illegal career. They'll probably shoot both of us, and Wolfie, too. Meredith moved up beside Mark and tried to read his face, but it was set like a stone, his eyes focused straight ahead. She thought of her mother and step-father, knowing they must be frantic over her whereabouts. For the second time since she climbed into the Cessna three days ago she regretted ever having left Baldwin Lake. But this time she was too scared to cry. *I'm going to die. We're all three going to die.*

Chapter Thirteen

Naoghi saw Maengun's ears prick up at the sound of the human's voice.

He seems to understand what he is hearing. And he doesn't seem to be alarmed, just surprised. There's much about him that I don't understand. But I do know that he is wiser and stronger than any of us. I hope we never lose him as leader.

"Come with me, Naoghi." Maengun turned in the direction of the human voice. "They're at the rendez-vous point." He bounded forward and began a fast-paced lope toward the meeting area. Naoghi followed suit, trying his best to keep up.

Does he actually want to encounter these humans? I sure hope not. They might shoot him the way they shot Tabar. Then I'd have to be leader again.

As they neared the rendez-vous, Maengun slowed his pace and stopped just short of the clearing. Naoghi stood beside him. Soon two other wolves joined them. Through the brush they could see a human crouched near the pups. Patanya stood with the pups growling, lips raised.

"We have to protect the young," one of the wolves said.

"I agree. We all know humans kill wolves." Naoghi reminded them.

The three pack wolves waited for Maegun's decision.

"We will do as Patanya is doing—threaten but do not attack. They have a firestick and will shoot any wolf that tries to harm them. Understood? Now walk out slowly, one at a time.

Maengun led the way. Naoghi let all the others precede him. Then he took his place beside the leader, bared his fangs, and snarled. The human backed away. It was then that he saw the other human figure standing at a distance. Hanging on his shoulder was the thing Naoghi feared the most—the firestick.

He's going to shoot one of us!

But the human did not remove the firestick from his shoulder. He stood perfectly still, speaking quietly to the female until she reached his side. Without warning Maengun sprang forward toward the human female. The male drew a blade from his side and rushed toward Maengun.

No, Maengun! Oh, no! Naoghi crouched, ready to spring to his leader's defense, when the female spoke in a loud voice to the male. He stopped but still held the blade. Naoghi's heart was pounding, his blood rushing. He wanted to attack but felt he must obey his leader's orders. Naoghi watched as Maengun stopped a few paces in front of the female. She held out her hand to him. What happened next confounded Naoghi. Maengun sniffed the hand, and the female embraced Maengun. He seemed happy to be with her. The alpha wolf joyfully licked her face then led her back to the pups. She touched them, gently caressing their ears, foreheads, and necks. Naoghi observed the scene in amazement and disbelief. *This is really strange. Yet Maengun understands human. He wouldn't endanger our only young ones, or any of the pack.*

The other two pack wolves backed away, tucked their tails, and returned to the forest, stopping every few feet to look back over their shoulders. Naoghi followed, but stood at the edge of the clearing, watching Maengun. After a while Patanya goaded the pups back into the brush. The two humans finally turned their backs and started walking away. Maengun gave a long and intense look at the watching wolf then ran to catch up with the human couple.

I will return, but be watchful. At least that's what Naoghi thought Maengun's eyes had said. He started back after the pack. But something made him stop. An inner voice, an instinct. Naoghi shivered. *He is going to need me.*

He turned around, saw the alpha wolf and two humans disappear into the bush on the far side of the rendez-vous clearing, lowered his body, and crept after them.

* * *

Maengun felt sure Naoghi could take responsibility for the pack until he returned from escorting Meredith and her friend a short way. He just couldn't leave her yet. He wanted to run with her for old times' sake. He relished feeling her hands on his head and ears once again. He needed to walk beside her a little longer. He was conflicted. He yearned to rediscover his life with humans, but the call of the wild was strong in his heart. He had responsibilities—to Patanya and the pups and to the pack. They all needed him, they all depended on him. He led them, and he loved them. He would return to them.

Humans are slow. But I guess they don't use speed to protect themselves—they have weapons that can kill predators. Without their guns they are weak and vulnerable. But Meredith never had a weapon, did she?

Maegun glanced at Meredith, then at her companion.

Just as I thought. He has a rifle. He can protect them both.

Maengun picked up the scent of meat, large animal meat. He left the two humans to follow the aroma, running straight ahead along the path. Reaching the body of the beheaded moose, he stopped, listening and looking for any sound or sight of human hunters. This was not an animal kill. Some of the meat had been torn away by a hawk or another large bird of prey, but not even a large bear could cut off a head.

Maengun walked cautiously over to the carcass, sniffed and tasted.

I must tell Naoghi and the others about this as soon as I get back. The meat is fresh enough to eat, and there is plenty of it here to feed us all.

Maengun felt conflicted again. He hated humans for killing animals of the wild, but he didn't hate Meredith or her family or her companion. And hunters had on occasion supplied the pack with an ample meal. He took another bite of the meat, swallowed a large chunk, then sat back, and thought.

What if the hunters are still in the area? They could hurt my human friends or one of the wolves. I must see to this now.

He ran back up the trail to warn Meredith. He found her and her friend standing close together, their arms around one another, their faces touching. Circling their legs didn't seem to get any attention.

Instincts urged Maengun to run ahead and try to stop the hunters before they could do any more harm. His blood was up, his teeth were set to kill if necessary. Despite the free meals, forest dwellers loathed the hunters and feared their guns. Many of them feared all humans, unable to distinguish the good from the bad, incapable of realizing that it was the weapons, not the humans, that kill.

He stopped to listen. In the distance he could hear the sound of a human voice and the *swish* of something large being dragged along the path.

The severed head, an inner voice told him.

The hunters are on the path ahead of us, moving in the same direction, but much more slowly. I must overtake them before Meredith and her friend do.

Glancing back, Maengun could see the two young people making steady progress down the trail. He ran on, stopping to listen and sniff the wind now and then to make sure he was on the right track. As the odor of the hunters grew stronger and the voices became louder, Maengun's anger intensified. His lips curled up. His throat tightened, ready to growl. Saliva dripped from his gums.

These men are not ordinary hunters. There is something about them. Something wrong.

Inner voices were screaming in his head. But he had heard enough. He would try to frightened them off. If they didn't run, he would attack, and he would kill. He wished he had the pack with him. It would insure his success in dealing with these brutes.

The dragging sound stopped. The footsteps as well. Maengun crept lower, his underside just above the forest floor. Through the foliage he could see two men sitting on the ground. Next to one stood a large bag which Maengun was sure contained the moose head.

Best to surprise them.

He waited in a thicket of berry bushes for the right moment to show himself. When one of the men, a tall thin one, stood up, the wolf sprang toward him.

"God, Manny, it's a wolf! Shoot him!"

The other human froze. Eyes wide, he didn't seem to hear what the tall one said. The tall man bent to pick up a rifle from the ground. Maengun let out a fierce growl and faked the start of a spring. The man grabbed the rifle and backed up. He cocked the rifle and aimed. He was ready to fire.

"Drop your weapon." Maengun recognized the voice of Meredith's companion behind him.

Chapter Fourteen

Brad had no trouble finding the empty Cessna again and moored the Otter next to it. Nor did Bobby have any trouble leading them to the aboriginal campsite. He simply followed the markings he had left for Meredith.

"No sign anyone's been here since yesterday," Paul was quick to observe.

"I'll check inside. She may have left a note." Bobby ducked into the tent.

Karen was awed by all she saw—the fire pit with its cauldron, the hanging food bundles, the carefully constructed drying racks, the old-style wigwam. She could hear a rippling sound.

"There must be a stream nearby. Of course," she said more to herself than to Paul or Bobby in the tent. Following the sound and an obviously human-made trail, she came to the water. The unusually dry summer had reduced it to a trickle, but enough to sustain life.

The campsite is well-chosen. Meredith's native friend must be quite skilled at survival. The thought gave her comfort. Back at the campsite she found Bobby, Paul and Brad ready to head out.

"No one's been here since yesterday, Karen," Bobby said, agreeing with Paul's observation. "We'll just have to search. Maybe you had rather stay here in case they come back."

"No. I want to look for her. I've stayed behind and waited too long already."

"Okay. But you don't have a gun, so you'll need to stay close and walk between us. Be very careful. Watch your footing. If you think you hear something or see something, we'll all go to investigate. We have to stay together.

"How do you know which way to go?"

"There seem to be three paths converging on the camp. The one we came in on, the one beyond the firepit . . ."

"That one just leads to a small stream," Karen interrupted her husband.

"The camp water supply," Bobby said, thinking aloud. "Then we'll take the one behind the tent. It seems to head north."

"To the wolves, no doubt," Brad said.

Karen still couldn't believe this was happening. Now both of her children were exposed to the dangers of the wilderness—her teenage daughter and her unborn child.

Bobby is right. I must walk carefully. Since the men were carrying the provisions in backpacks and each had a rifle, she could travel the path unencumbered and pay attention to every step.

"Before we leave I'd like to peek inside the wigwam. I might find a clue." She just wanted to find some evidence of her daughter. Her instincts would tell her whether or not Meredith had been there.

"Okay, take a quick look, but we need to hurry." Karen noticed the reluctant tone of Bobby's "okay."

Pulling open the bark flap that covered the tall arched entry, she stepped inside. The coziness of the interior pleased her. Whoever stayed here was organized. Books were stacked neatly beside a bearskin pallet, a plate and various utensils lay on crude split-log shelves. A lantern sat on the floor next to a folding chair. Karen was relieved to see that there were no signs of a struggle. Meredith must have come here willingly. Karen stared at the bed envisioning her innocent daughter lying in this bear-skin bed, a stranger's bed.

This is where she spent the second night . . . alone, I hope. Yes, alone, I'm sure. She's a good girl. And whoever is with her is good, too. I wonder if he killed and skinned the bear. Reassured by the atmosphere of the wigwam, Karen emerged determined to find Meredith and the stranger.

"Let's go get her." Karen managed to smile at the men waiting for her.

With Bobby in front and Brad and Paul behind her, Karen could concentrate on securing her footing and keeping pace with her husband. The path veered slightly east toward the lake. Within a few minutes she could see water sparkling through the trees. Reaching the shore they found a small motor boat moored to a tree stump that had been notched at the rear to hold the rope firmly in place.

"His fishing boat." Bobby seemed to think he was obliged to explain everything. He walked over for a closer look. "It's seen a lot of use."

That's very interesting, but since Meredith is not in it, let's keep going. Karen did not want to lose the momentum of the search or her positive frame of mind. She folded her arms and waited, hoping, by the expression on her face and an audible sigh, to communicate her eagerness to move on. Bobby got the message.

"I think the path continues north, this way." He took the lead again.

They moved as quickly as possible through the thick underbrush and deep footing until they approached a small ravine. Bobby spotted a rope attached to a tree limb that projected out over the depression.

"They haven't come back or the rope would be on this side."

Thank you, dear, for your explanation. "Then I guess we have to climb down and back up." Karen would have enjoyed swinging on the rope, under different circumstances.

"Hold on to me, Sweetheart. We'll take it slow and easy."

She was happy for Bobby's assistance. Maneuvering the ravine proved harder than she had thought and left her a little out of breath. Bobby noticed, of course.

"Let's take a short break to get our bearings," he proposed.

While the men looked around for the continuation of the path, Karen sat on the ground and leaned back against the tree which held the looped swing rope. There were footprints in the dirt at the base of the tree. Lug soles.

"Meredith," she whispered and sprang to her feet with renewed vigor and determination.

"This way, Karen." Bobby was again in command of the brigade.

Although the going was rough at times, they made steady progress through the forest. Bobby stopped for a moment and turned to her.

"Hear that? Sounds like a waterfall off to the left." He turned back around and kept going straight.

Karen trusted Bobby's knowledge and skills in the wilderness world. No doubt he recognized various animal tracks along the way and kept his senses keen for any sign of a bear or bull moose.

By early afternoon Karen was famished.

"Bobby," she called, "can we stop for lunch?"

"I was just about to suggest it," he answered. "As soon as we find a place."

And they found a place, a place where someone had very recently built a fire. The odor of cooked meat hung in the air, and there were more lug-sole footprints. Paul spotted a folded tarp on the limb of a blue spruce.

"I think they must have spent last night here," he said. "Probably used the tarp as cover."

"You're right. Over there near the fire, against that embankment." Brad pointed.

One bed, one tarp. Karen was starting to worry again. *What in the world has my daughter gotten herself into?* She sighed as Bobby handed her a ham sandwich.

Karen sat down on the hillock in front of the remains of a fire. She didn't realize how hungry she was. The ham sandwich disappeared faster than a rabbit down a hole. Bobby twisted the cap off a plastic bottle of water, handed it to her.

"Where did they go from here?" she asked him.

"I'm not sure. There are several places that look like animal paths leading away from here. We'll check each one for evidence."

"You mean we've lost her trail."

"Temporarily."

"I just don't feel good about this anymore. I wish I knew who was with her."

"I think I do know."

"What? And you haven't told me? For heaven's sakes who?"

"I think I remember Tom mentioning the fact that his grandson had started spending several weeks each summer in the bush like he used to. Living the early native lifestyle. And I believe that Tom said he had helped him choose a remote place north of Baldwin Lake."

"So it might be him?"

"It's possible."

"I remember he had a grandson, but I don't know anything about him." Karen reached for Bobby's hand. "Oh, Bobby, if it's him, she'll be okay, won't she? I wish you had told me sooner. It's such a relief."

Bobby sat beside her and, still holding her hand, put an arm around her shoulders.

"I'm not one hundred percent sure. I didn't want to mislead you."

"Well, the important thing now is to discover where they went from here."

Karen took a final sip of water and stuffed the empty bottle into Bobby's backpack.

"Thanks for lunch. Let's get going, Bwana." Bobby stood and pulled her up.

It was mutually decided to follow the path to the northwest. Brad had noticed several broken branches on a small bush, and the floor looked more recently tamped down. Karen took one last look at the spot where her daughter had slept next to a stranger then stepped onto the path behind Bobby to begin the next leg of the journey.

Before long the path opened into a meadow-like area. Karen moved past Bobby and walked into the clearing.

"I smell wolves."

Bobby stepped to her side. "You smell what?"

"I know how Wolfie smelled. Especially in Meredith's room where he slept. And the wolf odor is too strong for just one wolf."

"The pack," Brad said. I can smell it, too."

"So do I," Paul said.

Bobby shook his head. "As long as I've dealt with the wilderness . . . . I can identify the tracks and the scat, but the odor . . . ."

"I take my kids to the zoo. They love the wolf section. That's how I recognize it," Paul explained.

"Okay, so Meredith found a wolf pack. But was Wolfie one of them?" Bobby wondered aloud.

Karen was more impatient than ever. "We can't answer that until we find her. Let's look for clues again. We're definitely gaining ground on them." She scanned the periphery of the clearing. Just as certain as the aroma of wolves came the sense that amber eyes were watching them.

* * *

Karen's heart beat faster. Her anxiety subsided as her hope rose. She knew she was getting closer to her daughter. She glanced around the clearing and tried to envision Meredith and her native companion meeting with the wolves. What if the wolves attacked? No, she decided. The native would not expose a girl to that possibility. And no doubt he was armed. She had seen boxes of shells in the wigwam, but no weapon. She prayed Meredith had found Wolfie, if for no other reason than to satisfy her curiosity concerning her pet's ability to adapt to the wilderness. Then perhaps she would forget about the wolf and get on with her life. What life? Wolfie was the main thing in her life, her principal joy year round. What did she have left? What could take Wolfie's place? For the first time Karen fully understood her daughter's desperate need to find the wolf. There was an enormous hole in the girl's existence that needed to be filled.

I will help her deal with this. Together, all three of us, we will find new people and activities for her. She'll be a senior this year. Surely there will be special events for her to participate in—and then, preparation for college. . . .

Bobby and Brad mutually decided that the two kids had taken a path south.

"They're probably heading back to the campsite," Bobby said. "This way may be a short cut back to the main path."

The trail was not easy to discern. Karen wondered how Bobby could tell which way to turn. But he led the expedition with confidence. A few broken twigs here and there reassured Karen that Bobby and Brad were right.

Bobby stopped. Karen followed his gaze to the trunk of a white pine.

"A bear sharpened his claws here."

Deep grooves striped the bark at eye level. In a few places whole chunks were missing. Karen's throat tightened.

"Do you think they're in danger?"

"Not really. These marks are not fresh. But there are bears around. There's always the risk of running into one. But they usually keep their distance."

Karen thought about the box of shells and the missing rifle. The two men with her were armed, and so was the one with Meredith.

"I am not going to worry about a bear. Let's keep going."

"Are you all right? Feeling okay? Do you need to rest?"

"Yes, I'm fine, no, I don't need to rest. I'll be a lot better when we locate Meredith."

"Just let me know when you need a break." Bobby ducked under some low branches, turned around and held them up for Karen. Brad and Paul were close behind.

Within a few minutes they rejoined the same path they had followed north.

"Okay. We're back on the main path. Going will be a little easier now," Bobby announced.

"Let's take that break now, Bobby. And I could use a drink of water."

He fished another bottle out of his pack. Karen drained it and wiped her lips on the sleeve of her jacket.

"Speaking of water, I can hear the falls. I bet you guys are right. They are headed back to the wigwam."

Hope rose another notch as Karen handed the empty bottle to

Bobby. For the second time that day, she managed to smile at the three men taking her to her daughter.

* * *

Manny stumbled up to Travis, the bagged head bumping along beside him.

"You gotta let these kids go. We'll be out of here and long gone before they can report us. We'll never see them again."

"You let me do the thinking. You just take care of the trophy," Travis snapped back without taking his eyes off his prisoners.

The boy kept a good pace. He certainly knew the woods. He was sure-footed, steady, and quiet. The girl had to work hard to keep up. The wolf stuck close to her, stopping now and then to turn around, bare his teeth at Travis, and let out a low growl.

"Come on, Wolfie, that's enough." The girl tried to keep him quiet.

The wolf snarled and his shoulders quivered, but he obeyed.

It's a trained wolf. Probably hers, Manny thought. *She could tell him to tear our throats out and he'd do it. He wants to do it.* Manny hiked the rifle on his shoulder and forged ahead. He was really tired from lugging the trophy, two rifles, and a backpack. The sight of water winking through the trees gave him a little impetus.

"Much farther to the canoe?" he asked Travis.

"Just keep walking."

A strong wind swept across the lake and pushed its way into the forest. Manny sat the bag down and pulled on his hood. The breeze brought fresh aromas of pine and spruce that for a moment blew away the putrid odor of the decaying moose head and gave Manny some relief.

"Everybody stop!" Travis yelled. "This way." With the muzzle of his rifle he indicated a well-concealed side path.

How the heck did he ever learn his way around up here? He knows hidden trails and the location of all the animals. He seems to have a sixth sense. Years of poaching, I guess. Manny picked up the moose head.

Except for his grunting as he lifted the bag over forest debris, they moved on in silence for a while.

The boy turned to face Travis.

"We're taking a break here. The girl needs to rest."

"Yeah? And I suppose the wolf needs to pee, too, huh? I know I do.

How 'bout you, Manny?" Travis began unzipping his fly.

"For God's sake, don't do that in front of the girl!" Manny glared at Travis.

"We're in the bush, pal." Travis' laughed, defiant and arrogant. "Just point your gun at her while I take care of business." He urinated on a small juniper bush, in full view. The girl turned away.

Manny hated himself for holding a weapon on these innocent kids. They just happened to be in the wrong place at the wrong time. He hated himself for being Travis' puppet. He'd rather have his gun trained on his so-called "partner." Only he'd likely be tempted to pull the trigger.

* * *

Naoghi found it easy to track Maengun and the uprights. The humans emitted a strong acrid scent that was unmistakable.

It's their skin. They have no fur covering it, he thought.

He was accustomed to following Maengun. His aroma was familiar. But there were other odors besetting his olfactory senses. *A moose, a dead moose. And other humans. Farther away.*

He flared his nostrils and drew several quick, strong breaths.

Marngun. And his human companions.

He stopped to listen. He heard one of the uprights' steady shuffle and Maengun's lively prancing. The steps of the other human farther away were barely audible.

Maengun is happy with these humans. I have never seen him like this. I thought he had forsaken his old life with them. Is he planning to go back? We need him, they do not. Perhaps he is tired of leading us. But he wouldn't leave Patanya and the pups.

Naoghi's mind was full of questions and doubts about the wisdom of Maengun's behavior, but his heart was full of courage. His instincts were driving him to follow them. Why, he did not know.

The hair suddenly bristled on the back of his neck. He thought he heard Maengun growl. Then, voices. With threatening tones. He felt his lips pulling back from his teeth. A low rumble came from his throat. He sank even closer to the ground, but continued tracking.

Danger. Maengun and his human pack are in danger.

Naoghi had been following them out of curiosity. Now something stronger was compelling him. Something sinister. His chest and shoulders quivered. He raised up and loped ahead, nose flaring. He now understood his mission. His eyes and ears became sharper, just as they did during a kill with the other wolves. With renewed vigor he trailed the humans the way he would a prey.

The scents of Maengun and the uprights suddenly disappeared. Naoghi stopped, lifted his muzzle and sniffed. They definitely had not come this way. He would have to backtrack and pay closer attention. In his eagerness to catch up, he had somehow missed a turn, and that added to his growing sense of alarm.

"I've got to find them before it's too late," he whimpered to himself. "Too late for what?" He didn't know and didn't have time to think about it now.

Turning, he loped back up the path with his senses on full alert.

"Here!"

He had reached an old trail to the water where the aromas were unmistakable. With his blood roiling, he took the side path.

"An upright's body water," Naoghi identified the pungent odor emanating from a juniper tree. He knew he was getting closer. For some reason this bitter smell lent a sense of urgency to his pursuit. He quickened his pace down the path.

Low rumbles emerged from his throat. He bared his teeth. His full trot became an all-out run, as though he were overtaking a caribou or an elk. His heart pounded in his ears. Saliva flew from his parted lips. Instinct alone propelled him now.

As he neared the water he could hear voices and the shuffling of the uprights feet. He slowed to a walk, lowered his body, and crouched behind a clump of shoreline bushes. Instinct told him to wait until it was his time to act.

* * *

During the forced march Mark formulated a plan. When they reached the ravine he would grab the rope with one hand, Meredith with the other, and swing both of them across. Then while the poachers were clambering down one slope and up the other, they could make a fast get-away. They men would not leave their bag with the trophy, so they had no chance of pursuing them, or at least of catching them. Mark knew several good hiding places in the woods between the path and his camp. He and the girl would wait it out until the poachers gave up and left the lake. No doubt a floatplane was scheduled to pick them up. He would hear it land and take off. Then they would be safe.

He hated to lose the rifle his grandfather had given him, but he had to protect the girl. If it were just himself, he would take the risk and try something more daring, like jumping on the lead man and wrestling the gun away from him. The bag man seemed harmless, even innocent. Yet he was poaching.

Unfortunately the turn off the main path had rendered his plan useless. They would not cross the ravine. Mark knew this side path to the lake. He had used it several times for duck hunting, but he had not expected the poachers to take it. They would arrive at the lakeshore soon. He had to come up with an idea fast.

That low-life will never let us go. He intends to kill us both. Probably the wolf, too—as a second trophy. Otherwise why would he keep us with him?

In spite of the cool breeze off the water, perspiration ran down Mark's face. He was afraid, and he was angry. He gritted his teeth and half-closed his eyes. He thought of Gitchi-Manitou, the God of all creation, the Great Spirit, and prayed silently. Surely the Great Spirit and the spirit of his brother moose would come to his aid.

Great Spirit, you have seen the wrong done to one of your creatures, the dishonor heaped upon him. You are the master of all the forest. Send us your aid. Rescue us from these men who have shown such disrespect for your creation. I am sure they mean us harm. Protect us, especially Mni-Ha-Ha, whose life I value above my own.

Mark's pace had slowed during the prayer.

"Keep moving, boy!" the skinny guy yelled. Mark heard him unshoulder the rifle. The skin on the back of his neck crawled. He narrowed his eyes and swatted at a tangle of vines.

For the first time in my life I think I could kill a human being. And I will, if he tries to hurt Meredith . . . or even the wolf. I'll strangle him with my bare hands.

They were nearing the water. He could hear the slapping of waves against the shore. He could smell the plankton and the subtle piscatorial aroma of the lake. His arm muscles twitched. He would have to act soon, do something to save them. But what?

* * *

The going wasn't easy. Meredith had to concentrate to keep up with Mark. She knew a gun was aimed at the back of her head. Any second now a bullet could take her out. Her throat tightened and she wanted to cry. But from somewhere in her inner core an emotion more powerful than fear emerged and spread through her mind and body: she was angry. She hated these men for intruding on the joy and excitement fate had handed her so unexpectedly in the middle of the wilderness. She had found Wolfie. She had found Mark, or rather he had found her. This was her first great adventure, by far the most thrilling part of her life, and, she realized, her first romance. She refused to let these criminals ruin it. She had to do something, and do it herself. There was no way to confer with Mark, not without risking their lives.

Threading her way though bushes and stumbling over deep footing, she took stock of the situation, just as she had in the stranded floatplane.

There are two of them and two of us. They have three guns, we have none. But we have a wolf. We are younger. Mark knows the forest better than either of them. They are slowed by the bag with the moose head.

Her foot caught on a vine and she went down on both hands and one knee. Mark hadn't noticed her fall. In any case, he didn't stop.

"Get up!" The man with the gun waited while she righted herself and checked for any damage to her clothing. She hurried to catch up with Mark, took a deep breath, and continued her mental assessment.

The guy with the bag. I don't think he would hurt us. Yet he'll do whatever the guy with the gun tells him—but surely not kill us. The other one, he's as dangerous as he is disgusting. He's not going to let us go alive. Somehow we've got to get the rifles away from him before he reaches the shore or else we're doomed. We won't stop them from leaving with their trophy—after all, the moose is dead. I've got to find a way to get a rifle. If only Mark could help me. Or Wolfie.

Meredith could see the lake ahead. Only a few more steps and they would emerge onto the shore. She felt helpless.

They are going to kill us. Our only hope is to beg for our lives. Her heart pounded against her chest.

Mark was first to come out of the bush, Meredith and Wolfie followed.

"You kids pull the canoe out of the brush." The gaunt man motioned with the muzzle of the rifle. He indicated a clump of wilting greenery. Meredith went with Mark to the canoe and helped him remove the camouflage. Wolfie stayed at her side.

"I'm going to try to get the rifle away from him," Mark whispered.

"Then what?"

There was no time for an answer.

"Pull it out and get it into the water." Again the rifle waved directions.

Mark did as he was told.

"Wait. Let me put this bag in there first." The other man came forward dragging the severed head. He looked worn out as he tried to lift the bag. Mark came around to help.

"Thank you."

The words brought a little relief to Meredith. *He really is basically a nice guy. I know he won't hurt us. Maybe he'll talk the other one into letting us go.*

The nice guy and Mark got the canoe into the water.

"Go ahead. Get in and pick up a paddle," the skinny one said to his cohort. "We're going back to the pick-up spot." He glanced at his watch. "And we're right on time, too, buddy. Plane will be here soon. But first I have to take care of some unfinished business. The wolf, then the boy, then the girl."

He raised the rifle, pointed it at Wolfie, and pulled the trigger.

"No!" Meredith screamed and rushed toward Wolfie at the same time the gun fired.

A flash of brown and black fur flew past Meredith. She closed her eyes, not wanting to see Wolfie hit. Another shot expoded.

She opened her eyes. "Oh my God! Mark!" A wolf lay bleeding to her left. On her right the skinny man lay half in the water, half on the shore. The other man was standing in the canoe, a rifle in his hands. Before she could grasp what had happened, Mark had her in his arms.

"We're okay. We're okay, Mni-Ha-Ha."

Meredith released all the emotion of the past few hours, sobbing into Mark's chest.

"But Wolfie . . . He shot Wolfie."

"No, look." Mark turned her to face the water. "He's over there making sure the bad guy is not going to get up."

Meredith could see her wolf pulling at the man's jacket. She heard his low growl.

"Then what . . . ?"

"Another wolf ran between Wolfie and the gunman. Come on."

They walked over to the slain wolf.

"It's probably one of the pack."

"He took the bullet instead of Wolfie."

"Looks that way."

Mark bent down and touched the wolf's neck to feel for a pulse. "He's gone."

Wolfie trotted up and began to sniff and lick his pack brother—his muzzle, his ears, his eyes. Then Wolfie sat down beside the body.

"Are you kids okay?" The nice guy joined the mourners at the wolf's side.

Mark was the one to answer.

"That was a brave thing to do. You saved our lives."

"Not the wolf's though." He peered over the body.

Meredith looked from the dead wolf to the man who shot his partner. "This is *my* wolf." She put her hand on Wolfie's head. "His brother wolf saved him. I knew you wouldn't hurt us. We both knew. You're a good person. Thank you."

"Well, now I'm a murderer, not to mention the poaching."

"You shot to defend us. That's not murder. Don't worry. We'll vouch for you."

The roar of a plane drowned out the last of Mark's words. The good guy raised his voice.

"Someday I hope to get the chance to explain everything to you. Right now, we've got to get Travis into the canoe and back to the floatplane."

The three of them left Wolfie to mourn his friend and walked over to the body at the water's edge.

Again Mark checked for a pulse. "He's still alive. So you're not a murderer."

Travis groaned and tried to sit up. "Damn you!" was all he could manage to utter.

"I'll get him," Mark said. He was able to shoulder the thin man, walk to the canoe, and drop him in—none too gently.

The man got into the canoe with his wounded partner and picked up a paddle.

"I'm really sorry, kids, for what we put you through. And I'm sorry about the wolf. . . and the moose. It was all a big mistake."

"It's okay. We'll help you clear it up with the authorities," Mark said.

"My name is Meredith Marsten. You can reach me at Baldwin Lake Lodge. My dad owns it. We really want to help you."

The man looked at Meredith then lowered his eyes. He was at a loss for words.

Meredith would always remember the sorrow in the face of this man who saved her life and the life of her first love.

She and Mark stood by the water watching the canoe disappear around the shoreline. Meredith turned to her friend.

"Can you chant something for the wolf?"

"I can and I will."

Chapter Fifteen

When Maengun saw Meredith and the boy pull the canoe out of the bushes, he was afraid they would be leaving with the killing men. That was not good. He sensed Meredith's fear of the men, especially the one with the firestick. *He intends to harm them.*

With the boy's help, the other man swung the bag into the boat and got in. *But that one does not.*

Maengun sniffed the air. There was a faint odor of wolf. *Which wolf?* He drew several deep, quick breaths. *Naoghi. He has followed us and is nearby.* Maengun turned his head, looking up and down the tree line and inhaling, trying to locate the other wolf by sight or scent. He heard the tall, thin man say something. He swung around and saw the firestick aimed directly at him.

Everything happened fast. Maengun crouched to spring at the man. At the moment of the shot something bounded in front of him. A body fell no more than a tail's length away. Immediately another firestick went off. The tall man buckled and fell. The firestick flew out of his hands. Two bodies lay motionless. One wolf, one human. Maengun stood still for a few seconds expecting to hear more gunshots, but none came.

Anger propelled him toward the man lying at the water edge. He was the evil one who wanted to harm all three of them. When Maengun reached the body, a wildness possessed him. He sank his teeth into the clothing, pulled at it and shaking his head viciously. He would have liked to tear the man apart. Furious growls rose from his throat.

When he realized the man could do no more harm, he released his hold. An urgent instinct drove him back toward his brother. He ran full out but slowed to a trot as he neared. Head down, he approached with respect. Nosing up to the wolf lying in front of him, he licked his face to awaken him. No response.

In soft low tones Maengun spoke to his brother. "Naoghi. Don't let your spirit leave. Stay. The pack needs you. I need you." He sat and waited. No response. The eyes were clouding over.

He tried licking more vigorously, the eyes, the ears, the throat. Still no response. He inhaled. Naoghi's aroma was changing into something that Maengun recognized from the many creatures he had killed. The spirit wolf had left the earth wolf. The earth wolf had begun its return to the earth, but the spirit wolf lingered.

"Stay near, spirit of Naoghi. As long as I am alpha of the White Moon Pack, we will honor you, the bravest of us all." In a series of low whimpers he mourned his lost friend. He was vaguely aware that humans stood near in sympathy.

When Maengun looked up, Meredith and her wilderness friend were helping load the body of the fallen man into the canoe. He thought of running to Meredith but decided to stand at his bother's side. While the three of them watched the canoe disappear up the shoreline, the sound of an approaching motor diverted his attention.

The roaring bird. It brought me here and took my human family away. I hope it will take these men away so they won't harm any more forest dwellers.

Maengun's memory of the roaring bird had become dim, but he knew that it brought uprights and also took them away. He felt far removed from his old human life. He was even starting to feel removed from Meredith.

The roaring bird barely slowed to pick up the two hunters who abandoned the canoe. Just as it taxied out of sight, something moved in the bushes. Maengun flared his nostrils and sniffed the air. *More humans are coming through the forest.* For a moment his fur bristled. *No. These uprights are good. Her mother and father.* He felt relieved that his human friend would soon be in the protection of her family, but he also felt conflicted. Somehow she belonged here. She was learning wilderness ways, just as he had done earlier in the warm season. He took a last look at her standing beside the young human forest dweller.

Yes, the wilderness is in her blood now, as it is in mine. She will return. But she has another now. Someone to be with her and watch out for her when she comes back. She won't need me.

Although this thought saddened the wolf, it also relieved him of an almost forgotten responsibility. He had other obligations now. Patanya, the pups, the pack. The thought of his wolf family stirred his blood.

I must go to them and tell them about Naoghi's noble sacrifice. I will explain how he was with me from the beginning, how he taught so many of the ways of the forest, how he covered for so many of my early mistakes.

For some time now Maengun sensed that the warm season was

coming to an end. The pack needed to prepare for the cold.

We have hunting to do before the white season comes. The pups still have much to learn if they are to survive and become great hunters. Patanya and my brothers are waiting for me.

He glanced toward the forest, raised his muzzle, and inhaled. The aromas of the spruce and pines, the junipers and the choke cherries filled him with an inner peace, a deep joy, and made him turn from the uprights. He slipped quietly into the bush. As he trotted back along the path, the chirping of the boreal chickadees, the rustling of the gray jays, and the soft sounds of the small creatures of the forest floor lifted his heart, his full-fledged wolf's heart.

* * *

The crack of a gunshot cut through the profound silence of the wilderness. Before Karen had time to react, another shot pierced the stillness. Her pupils zoomed open to the max and her breathing stopped. In the split second it took her to realize what she had heard, fear flooded her body.

"Oh, my God! Bobby, those were gunshots."

"Stay here with Brad and Paul. I'll find out what's going on."

"No, I'm coming with you."

"Don't worry. They're probably hunting and shot a rabbit or something. But it's dangerous. You could get hit. "

Karen ignored his command.

Bobby moved thorough the bush like a predator on the chase, seemingly unmindful of the difficult footing and the impassability of the trail. Karen, Brad, and Paul kept up.

Karen no longer saw obstacles. Briars, thorns, and sharp twigs tore at her clothing through the thick brush. She traveled by instinct, oblivious to the scratches on her hands and face. There were no thoughts in her head, only purpose, instinctive purpose. She was the bull moose, she was the wolf.

Everything was happening at once. She heard the motor of an approaching plane. Straight ahead she saw brightness and the glimmer of water. They had reached the lake and a plane was landing. There were figures moving around, human figures.

Bobby whirled around to Karen and held up his two palms, signaling for the rescue party to stop. Then he lowered his palms to face the ground indicating they were to crouch down. The four of them took positions behind the shoreline shrubs.

A small cove sheltered an irregular beach no more than ten meters at its widest point. Two figures and a wolf stood on the beach. Karen squinted. A young man and a girl. Karen touched Bobby's arm.

"It's them," she whispered. "And a wolf."

He nodded. "Two wolves. One on the ground."

Karen didn't wait for any more signals from Bobby. The next thing she knew, she was running toward the girl with no concern for her own safety.

"Meredith, it's Mama!"

The girl wheeled around and, after an instant, with a look of total shock, ran into her mother's arms.

"Mama, you found me! How . . . ?" She began to sob.

"Nevermind that now, Sugar Baby. We're here to take you home."

Karen leaned back to gaze at her daughter, to take in the reality of her presence.

"Mama, your face is all scratched up."

"I've seen you looking better, too." She smiled.

"Muffin." Bobby said softly.

Karen released her daughter and stepped back to allow the reunion of father and daughter.

"Daddy." Meredith buried her face and arms in his chest. "I'm so sorry."

"Shh, now. Tell us who this young man is. I think I recognize Wolfie."

Mark stepped forward and held out his hand.

"Mr. Marsten, I'm Mark, Tom Redcloud's grandson."

"I thought that's who you were." Bobby put his free hand on the young man's shoulder as they clasped hands.

"Thank you for helping our girl."

"I think it's the wolf you need to thank."

"Wolfie?"

"No, sir. The other one." Mark turned toward the body.

"What in the world happened here? Did that wolf attack you?" Bobby asked. "We heard gunshots."

"It's a long story, Mr. Marsten. First let's get back to my campsite. Then Meredith can tell you everything—from the beginning."

* * *

Meredith stood leaning into her mother's arms, allowing the anxiety and fear of the past three days to dissolve. The magnitude of her ordeal began to dawn on her. She still couldn't believe that they had searched for her, risked so much to find her. She was embarrassed that SAR had to be called in, but she was grateful. Looking up at her mother's face she could see beyond the scratches to the fatigue brought on from worry and physical exertion.

"Mama," she whispered, "I'm not the same girl who left Baldwin Lake." Somehow she knew her mother understood what she meant.

"Life is changing for us all, Sugar. But Bobby and I will tell you about that once we are back at the lodge, safe and rested."

"Can you make another twenty-minute hike, Mrs. Marsten? To my camp? I'll make you some hot tea when we get there."

"Yes, I can. And the tea would be greatly appreciated." She stroked Meredith's hair and kissed her temple.

"What shall we do about the dead wolf's body?" Meredith asked.

"Leave it. Nothing goes to waste in the wilderness. What the bears don't consume, the eagles, ospreys, and gulls will. This wolf will continue giving himself to others."

"It's a beautiful pelt," Karen added.

"Yes, it is. And normally I would skin him and take it with me. But out of respect for this brave brother, I will leave him in the care of nature. He was a good friend to Wolfie. Which reminds me, there is something I need to do."

Meredith watched him walked to the body of the slain wolf and heard him began a soft chant."

In the surprise and excitement of the rescue and reunion with her parents she had forgotten about Wolfie. She scanned the beach but didn't see him anywhere.

"Wolfie? Wolfie, where are you, boy?"

She left Karen's side and started checking the shoreline bushes.

Mark finished the incantation and walked over to her.

"Did you see where Wolfie went?"

"I think he headed home—back to the pack."

"No, surely not yet! I didn't get to tell him goodbye."

"Mnihaha. It's time to let him go."

She turned toward him to protest, but the softness in Mark's eyes and the assurance in his voice convinced her. She closed her eyes. *He is so right.*

"It is. And I will." Despite the ache of loss in her heart, she smiled at her wonderful companion, her special one.

* * *

The slow trek back to the camp was complicated by the size of the party. Meredith knew that Mark would make sure they all got safely through the bush. She tried to picture him skinning a wolf and remembered turning away when he worked on the breakfast rabbit.

I could watch him skin animals, maybe even help him. It's all part of survival. It's nature's way. I could probably learn to cook the meat and eat it. But I could never, ever, kill a wolf."

As they made their way back Meredith thoughts rambled on about wilderness life. She tried walking the way Mark had shown her and found it easier now. Out of necessity she had become much more adept in moving through the bush. Moccasins. Back home she would practice with moccasins. Home. Something wet fell on the back of her hand. She reached up to her face and wiped away a streak of tears. But they kept coming. She wanted to go home with Karen and Bobby. She loved them both so much. And she loved her life at Baldwin Lake and in Winnipeg. She loved visiting her grandparents in South Carolina and Iowa. It was the life she had always known. But now . . . something else had taken root in her heart. Summer with Mark in the wilderness. She realized that was why she was crying. She would have to leave him, leave him alone in the wilderness, and go without the overwhelming joy his presence infused. Her heart was divided. She wanted to go, but she wanted to stay.

"Okay, let's stop here for a minute," Mark called out.

They had reached the ravine.

* * *

Mark used a single-burner butane camping stove to prepare raspberry tea. Meredith got out the camp chair for her mother then served her the tea in a tin cup. The hot tea seemed to restore her mother's spirit. She and Mark sat on the ground while Bobby and the two pilots found satisfactory logs. Meredith told her story, from that fateful morning when she left Baldwin Lake to the departure of the poachers' canoe. Mark filled in his part. Neither of them mentioned the shower at the waterfall, and they minimized the details of the sleeping arrangements in the north.

"You kids were very brave," Brad said.

"And very lucky," Paul added.

Karen was slow to respond. She just sat gazing at her daughter.

"I think you two have developed a special relationship."

Mark lowered his head. Meredith flushed.

Mama knows.

Bobby stood, picked up the empty tin cup, and walked over to Mark. "Thank you, son. I want you to know that you're welcome to come to the lodge anytime."

Bobby knows.

"We'd better start back to the plane. I want to get these people home and get myself back to Winnipeg before dark," Brad said.

Paul and the SAR man may know, too. I guess it shows. But that's fine.

* * *

Mark led the party back to the beach where the Otter and the Cessna were moored. Karen and Bobby said their final thank-you's and goodbyes to Mark and boarded the Otter. The pilots waited for Meredith.

"Take care of yourself, Mnihaha." Mark favored her with a final knee-weakening smile.

"And you do the same, Nagweyaab." Meredith looked at the ground for a moment mustering her courage. "Will I see you again?"

The presence of her parents impressed on her the reality of their disparate lives and cast a shadow on their intimacy. Their heart, soul, and, yes, body connection now seemed like a dream dissipated by the dawn.

Mark stepped toward her and took both of her hands. His eyes held hers for a moment and spoke more than words could ever. He pulled her closer, kissed her cheek.

"If that's what you want," he whispered. "We will be together again in the forest . . . someday."

"I'd like that."

Mark released her hands and stepped back. Meredith turned away quickly and started toward the plane.

I was crying when he first saw me. I don't want him to see me like that again.

Boarding the plane she wouldn't let herself look back. She settled in the rear seats with Karen and Bobby, leaving the cockpit for the pilots. Her eyes were a blur of tears during the taxi and take-off. As they gained altitude, she glanced down at the lake one last time. Wolfie's lake, Mark's lake, her lake . . . someday.

* * *

That night the White Moon Pack wailed for their lost brother then celebrated Maegun's return in joyous chorus.

* * *

That night, somewhere in the deep recesses of her wilderness dreams, Meredith howled with them.

If you enjoyed *Meredith's Wolf*, you will probably want to read Judith's debut novel, *Poplar River*.

Karen Kingsley and her husband have been given a honeymoon trip to Poplar River in the Canadian wilderness by her husband's cousin, Bobby. Karen immediately finds herself at home in the wild and develops into an expert fisherwoman who looks forward to returning to Poplar River. But all is not well with Karen, despite the birth of a daughter and musical skills that bring her more offers than she can accept. She loses twin sons, then finds her husband mysteriously depressed. In a sort-of reverse *Dr. Doolittle*, Karen's encounters with the animals of Poplar River are first told through her eyes, then through the eyes of the animals who tell their sides of the stories. From ThomasMax Publishing, $13.95 in print, $5.99 in Kindle or Nook e-book format.

www.ingramcontent.com/pod-product-compliance
Lightning Source LLC
Chambersburg PA
CBHW020129180626
46810CB00004B/1475